LUMBERJACK

ANTHONY ENGEBRETSON

Cover Art & Illustrations by Jonathan LaMantia

Edited by Alex Woodroe

Content warnings are available at the end of this book. Please consult this list for any particular subject matter you may be sensitive to.

Published by Tenebrous Press.
Visit our website at www.tenebrouspress.com.

First Printing, December 2023.

The characters and events portrayed in this work are fictitious. Any similarity to real persons, living or dead, is coincidental and not intended by the author.

Print ISBN: 978-1-959790-96-9
eBook ISBN: 978-1-959790-97-6

Cover art and illustrations by Jonathan LaMantia.

Edited by Alex Woodroe.

Formatting by Lori Michelle.

Selected Works from Tenebrous Press:

Posthaste Manor
a novel by Jolie Toomajan & Carson Winter

The Black Lord
a novella by Colin Hinckley

Dehiscent
a novella by Ashley Deng

House of Rot
a novella by Danger Slater

Agony's Lodestone
a novella by Laura Keating

Soft Targets
a novella by Carson Winter

Crom Cruach
a novella by Valkyrie Loughcrewe

Lure
a novella by Tim McGregor

One Hand to Hold, One Hand to Carve
a novella by M.Shaw

More titles at www.TenebrousPress.com

For Maggie,
In a world full of Nevilles, you filled our hearts with wild flowers

NOTES ON HISTORICAL ACCURACY

Caution: contains spoilers

First and foremost, *Lumberjack* is a work of fiction. While it draws from a historical time and place, the events depicted in this story did not happen. J. Sterling Morton and Joy Morton were real people, as was their family. But the Mortons depicted in this book are only fictionalized versions of the men who actually existed.

All of J. Sterling Morton's accomplishments mentioned in the story occurred: he was governor of the Nebraska territory, served on the administration of Grover Cleveland's second presidency, established a magazine called *The Conservative* and, of course, founded the American Arbor Day. His racist views depicted in this book were also pulled from historical fact. Yet I did not delve into the fullest extent of Morton's racism (e.g. his opposition to abolishing slavery), which has been discussed in detail by resources such as the Nebraska Historical Society and the very museum at Arbor Lodge dedicated to the man. For other character details, I drew largely from publicly available facts, including the death of his wife Caroline and youngest son Carl. But I won't claim that the man depicted in this book completely thinks, speaks, and behaves as the real life Morton did. It was not my intention to make a character that does so.

As for Joy Morton, he was indeed the name behind Morton Salt and would often spend summers at Arbor Lodge. Otherwise, I gathered fewer details about the actual man when creating this fictionalized depiction.

Arbor Lodge is a real place, located in Nebraska City that was built on the traditional lands of the Jiwere (Otoe) and the Očhéthi Šakówiŋ and not far from traditional lands of the Pâri (Pawnee).

ANTHONY ENGEBRETSON

Prior to writing this book, I visited the mansion. I tried to make it accurate to what it would have more or less looked like at the time of this story. Every room mentioned in the story, including the guest room where General Denver had stayed, would have been in the actual house. That said, I didn't agonize over making every single detail authentic and took many creative liberties for fiction's sake. For example, I sincerely doubt the painting of the Table Creek Treaty signing (which is real and as described in the book) would have actually fit on the east wall of the parlor. According to the museum in Arbor Lodge where the painting currently is displayed, it would have actually been in a library at the time this novella is set. J Sterling really went to Illinois to live with Joy around this time period until his death in 1902. Shortly thereafter, the house was renovated by Joy.

There was no Neville the "lumberjack". The character is entirely made up, based initially on a silly character from a college film I had made. The curse (or whatever it may be) was also entirely my fabrication. As far as I know, Arbor Lodge was never overtaken by prairie life. J. Sterling Morton was likely ailing at the time, but there is no evidence he would have been haunted by a mysterious creature. Nor was his estate under the care of a man named Thomas Dailey—also a fictional character. The unfortunate boy, William, and his gruesome death were also made up. As far as I know, no such murder had occurred in Nebraska City during this time.

I feel that the use of the real historical elements serves this story thematically. But this is not meant to provide an educational, true-to-life historical account. This story is, at the end of the day, a fantasy that mirrors reality—mostly in all the worst ways.

CHAPTER ONE

Nebraska City, Nebraska. April 1901.

H**E WOULD NOT** let go.

No matter how much his hands ached, Neville kept clutching his axe. He had no idea where he was being taken. The carriage driver said nothing, only quietly whistled a tuneless melody as they meandered through a corridor of trees. Alexander's silver head gleamed at the sight of these wooden titans, eager to chop into one, bring it hurtling toward the ground. The idea brought a tingle to Neville's groin, and his breathing became intense.

Even with this minor surge of arousal, his anxiety didn't subside. He kept his cramped hands firmly on Alexander's handle. They seemed to be going farther and farther from town. For all Neville knew, this corridor led to another world.

The driver's tuneless noise continued, accompanied by the early evening crickets. The man was either unaware or uncaring of Neville's anxiety. This bothered Neville.

He wanted to shout, to demand answers like a man was supposed to. But to his shame, his dry throat could barely utter a croak. He was just as dazed as he was scared. There was no way he could have anticipated this day turning out the way it did. He was supposed to be on a train by now, heading toward Minnesota. It was difficult to pinpoint what had gone wrong. All his mind could conjure were those massive yellow eyes, that animalistic stench, a malicious giggle echoing through the air. Were those eyes watching him now? The thought made his body go cold. He pulled Alexander closer to his chest.

The driver's song sounded like a butchered version of "Stars and Stripes Forever". The familiar tune pulled Neville back into the moment. He focused on the driver, on the man's short black hair. Who this man was, where they were going, who Mr. Morton was—that had precedence over the creature.

It embarrassed Neville to think how unquestioningly he had gotten into this man's carriage and let himself be taken away. But everything had happened so fast. When the Sheriff told him his bail was paid, Neville's first thought had been that somehow, his father already knew of his predicament, despite being thousands of miles away in San Francisco, and that his journey would be over. He had been certain then that he would be condemned to working in the museum again, polishing up artifacts from distant lands until he finally worked up the nerve to hang himself.

But then he left the sheriff's office to find a tall, slender, copper-skinned man—a native, Neville assumed, though he had never met one in person—waiting for him. With his worn work clothes and tattered old hat, the man looked almost as filthy as Neville was, but the carriage he stood beside was elegant and clean, pulled by a healthy grey horse.

"Come with me," the man had said, not even introducing himself. "Mr. Morton would like to meet you." He had a surprisingly deep voice, unfitting for such a narrow body. Neville was shorter, but no thinner, yet his own voice was high and nasally.

Neville shuddered with self-loathing. He should have demanded answers before getting into the carriage. Instead, he meekly did as he was told, following a strange man's orders like a good little boy. So disgusting. Neville had an urge to chop his own hand off. Only a true man deserved his hands. Perhaps his father had been right all along. With that thought, Neville fancied going further and cutting off his own head.

Before Neville's self-resentment could simmer further, the end of the corridor came into sight. There, standing proudly in the evening light, was a white house. It was two stories tall and wider than some of the finest mansions in San Francisco. The roof seemed broad enough to hold an entire garden. The house almost reminded Neville of ancient Roman temples with its multi-pillared facade. The windows were tall and extravagant, some gleaming with the bright luminescence of electric lighting. This was a palace.

"Here we are," the driver mumbled. "Arbor Lodge."

Neville's heart eased at the sight. This wasn't just wealth he was seeing, but power, the well-assured conquest of civilization over the elements.

Still, his head roiled with questions, and he couldn't loosen his grip on Alexander just yet. Who exactly was this Mr. Morton? Why did he help Neville? What did he want?

Stepping through the main door, Neville thought he would enter a magnificent foyer or a grand entrance hall. But instead, it led into a stifling hallway, dimly lit by electric lamps. The walls were smothered in a swampish green wallpaper, though the wallpaper itself could hardly be seen through the clutter of portraits and paintings. The air smelled strangely of grass and dirt.

The copper-skinned driver, leading Neville into the house, sniffed and contorted his face. Neville assumed the man was smelling the same thing until he said: "You need a bath."

Neville's gut clenched. "What?"

The driver continued down the hall, not bothering to look back at the guest. "Wash your clothes, too."

Neville stood aghast; he had half a mind to answer this insult with Alexander's blade. But when he sniffed his tan shirt, which had once been white, the stench made him recoil. It had indeed been a while since he'd bathed or washed his clothes. His discolored shirt and overalls, his black derby hat, boots and socks, and his stained undergarments were the only clothes he had left. He'd sold the rest during his journey. But was this not the stench of a man? A working man? The driver had no such stench, so what kind of man was *he*?

Neville grinned victoriously. The driver was free to cover his nose all he'd like, if a man's musk was too much for the poor boy. He amused himself by imagining the driver going back to his home, dousing his soft, delicate body in women's perfumes.

"Are you coming?" the driver shouted. He was well down the hall, standing beside a staircase leading up to the second floor.

Neville didn't realize he'd been standing at the entrance for some time, caught up in one of his "spells", as his mother called them. "Of course," he said, continuing down the hall.

Neville thought he heard the driver give a low sigh. He

supposed the last thing the man wanted to do with his evening was wait on strange, smelly men. But it seemed he was at the mercy of Mr. Morton's command.

Moving toward the driver, Neville passed a parlor. The room was large and open enough to fit ten people, even though it was adorned with fine furniture and a piano in a corner. The wallpaper was more of a lighter, tea green, much less suffocating than the swamp shade of the hallway. Within the parlor was another entryway leading into what appeared to be a dining room. Neville had little time to stop and appreciate the details as he could feel the driver's impatient gaze burrowing into him. After passing the parlor, he stood beside an entrance that gave him a better look into the dining room.

"Wait here," said the driver before jogging up the stairs. Neville grumbled. Why had the man been so insistent if he was just going to make him wait some more?

While he waited, he examined the dining room. A long table filled most of it. Much of the table was empty, dust coating its surface. It apparently hadn't served many people in a long time. Something about the house felt strangely empty, too. Neville would have expected a mansion like this to have a staff of at least four or five people. Come to think of it, why was the driver doing the job of a butler?

Everything was quiet but for two noises, the mumbling sounds that came from upstairs—no doubt the driver convening with Mr. Morton—and the sharp ticking of a grandfather clock in the corner of the dining room. The clock stood next to an oval stained-glass window depicting a tree and what appeared to be a family motto that Neville couldn't read. Something at the foot of the clock caught his eye. At first, he doubted it could possibly be what he thought it was; surely a mansion like this wouldn't be subject to such disorder. But it became clear that his eyes did not deceive him. It was a patch of brown grass poking through the floorboards. When the mumbling upstairs ceased, Neville heard a new sound. It seemed to come from directly beneath his feet, like the scratching of dozens of tiny claws, small creatures moving under the floor.

"Mr. Morton will see you in his room," the driver said as he descended the stairs. Stopping at the last step, the man motioned to Alexander. "Perhaps you would like to put your axe away first?"

A rush of fear shot through Neville's body and he squeezed Alexander to his chest.

The driver sighed. "Maybe you could leave it in the hall," he suggested, pointing up the stairs, "outside of Mr. Morton's room?"

Neville continued squeezing Alexander. The idea of his axe not only being out of his hands, but out of sight, was unthinkable. When the Sheriff had confiscated Alexander, he'd felt like he was going to die, that his heart would stop and he would drop dead on the cold cell floor. Never again. He shook his head profusely.

The driver visibly fought to keep his frustration as contained as possible. Before he could say anything else, a firm voice bellowed from upstairs. "Thomas, bring him."

There was a familiar, patriarchal air to that voice that sent chills through Neville's body. For all he knew, it may have been his father up there. He hugged Alexander tighter, only loosening his grip when the blade nearly cut into his neck.

"Very well," the driver, Thomas, said. He nodded for Neville to follow him back up the stairs. As they ascended, Thomas kept his hip slightly turned so that his back wasn't completely to Neville. Perhaps he felt safer that way. To have another man frightened of him, even slightly, gave Neville a twinge of pride. This empowering feeling gave him the courage he needed to move forward and face Mr. Morton.

The bedroom was humid and an almost bovine smell lingered in the air, which reminded Neville of that yellow-eyed fiend's stench. His brief bout of courage ended, and he felt a powerful urge to retreat, but what he saw on the large bed wasn't a monster. Nor was it his father, though the man sitting regally against the headrest bore a similar bushy mustache, thinning white hair, and even the same massive ears, lobes drooping to the neck. But while Neville's father was slender and loomed like a tree, a similar frame to Thomas, this man was stout and full. The differences seemed moot as soon as the man's serious eyes focused on Neville; the lumberjack felt paralyzed beneath the gaze.

"Him?" the old man asked. "This is him?" He was underwhelmed and made no effort to conceal it in his voice.

"In the flesh," Thomas said with a mocking air of grandiosity. "I apologize, Mr. Morton, he wouldn't part with his axe."

Mr. Morton shook his head. "It's no matter. Go get supper ready."

Thomas hesitated. "Are you sure?" he said.

Mr. Morton glared at him. The power of those eyes didn't seem to have any effect on Thomas anymore, but he didn't argue with them either.

"Fine then." Thomas began to take his leave.

Neville had no love for the unpleasant driver, but at this moment wished he would stay.

"Close the door," Mr. Morton ordered.

Thomas complied, closing the door behind him, leaving Neville alone with Mr. Morton.

A stillness came over the room. Everything was silent but for the small ticks of a clock in the corner. Neville tried to keep his eyes from meeting Morton's, which remorselessly burrowed into him. Yet, there was nowhere safe to look. All over the room, eyes were staring out at him: black and white photographs and elegant paintings of relatives. They smothered him as much as the sickly yellow wallpaper did. All tested Neville, waiting in silence for him to do what was expected. He wished to God he knew what that was. He would have done anything for some kind of hint.

But before he could release the steady scream building in his chest, the silence was finally broken by Mr. Morton. "Have a seat, why don't you?"

Neville was struck with a rush of relief. Compliantly, he sat in a chair beside the bed, but not before removing a magazine titled *The Conservative* from its seat.

"Mr. Dailey," Morton said once Neville was seated, nodding toward the door to indicate that he was referring to Thomas. "He is not the best help one can get. But he is the only one who remained." Morton's eyes mercifully released Neville as the old man frowned at the quilted sheets covering his legs. "I would have preferred to meet in a more formal setting, of course. But I'm afraid I am not feeling myself of late."

Neville said nothing. He could tell Morton's source of embarrassment had nothing to do with impressing Neville. He was embarrassed that a man like himself would be reduced to granting an audience to *anyone* from his bed.

"Now, then." Morton winced in pain as he shifted, his eyes again seizing Neville. "What is your name?"

"Neville Gibbons." He answered like an acquiescent child.

"Gibbons." Morton frowned, which made Neville feel as if this answer, though true, had been the wrong one. "And what brings you to Nebraska City?"

"I came for the train station," Neville said. "I'm on my way to Minnesota."

"And what is in Minnesota?"

"Work," Neville said, hoping Morton would leave it at that. But just as he feared, Morton asked him what kind of work he was looking for. Keeping his voice firm, he answered. "I am a lumberjack."

Morton nodded, his pasty skin flopping freely about his neck. His face betrayed no surprise nor, to Neville's astonishment, skepticism.

"Where are you from?" was the old man's next question.

"California," Neville said, hoping he would not have to specify the city.

"Surely there is an abundance of work for a lumberjack in California."

Neville felt sick. Despite this, he stated calmly: "I wanted a change in scenery."

He didn't want to explain how he had been thrown out of lumber camps in California, Oregon, and Colorado, how he wanted to get as far from his previous failures as possible and have a true start. Maybe Minnesota was where he was truly destined to be, and if that failed, perhaps he would go up to Ontario, land of Big Joe Mufferaw. He would find his place, the memories of his failures wouldn't sting any more, and the specter of his father would leave him be. But he didn't want to say any of this.

"A change in scenery," he reiterated when Morton's silence became too much. He wanted to hit himself for doing so, for surely now Morton would know there was more to it.

"Do you have any family?" the old man asked abruptly.

"Family?" Neville was ready to say no. No family, none. But there was a heavy note to Morton's voice that indicated a deep importance to this question. Perhaps Neville could tell the stories he made up in his head. His father had been a lumberjack, a great one, a Californian Mufferaw, whose pride in his son had been as towering as he was. But now he was dead. And Neville had no brothers. Yet he knew Morton would be immune to this tale.

"Yes, family." Morton said. He gave such an emphasis to the word, one would have thought he was speaking the name of God himself.

Neville had little choice but to tell the truth. Some of it at least. "I have a father and a mother. They live in California. I am the youngest of four sons."

At this, Morton's eyes lit up, and for the first time, Neville felt he'd said the correct thing.

"And your father," Morton said, "what does he do?"

He did not ask if Neville's father or brothers were lumberjacks. Perhaps he did not imagine they were. Unfortunately, there was little choice but to tell the truth. "My father is a museum director in San Francisco."

"And your brothers?" The questioning felt merciless.

"The eldest, Eric, is a college dean. Colin owns a bank. John is a priest." Neville clenched his teeth. Would he have to say more? Would he have to name Eric's college? Or say what seminary John had attended?

"And you have chosen to be a lumberjack," Morton said. "Why?"

Neville felt like a condemned man having to explain himself to a judge. He squeezed Alexander tight. The little clock continued its impatient ticking.

"Because," he said, swallowing to moisten his throat. "Because I—I wanted to—I . . . " Why was his mind failing him now? It felt like every thought was frozen in ice; he could hardly remember his own name.

"Do you know who I am?" Morton asked.

Changing the subject was a true act of mercy that Neville was grateful for, but he resented the stuttered mess Morton had reduced him to. To the man's question, he shook his head.

Morton didn't seem disappointed by this. On the contrary, he was more than happy to explain. "Had you spent more time in Nebraska, you surely would have heard my name. I am Julius Sterling Morton. I have committed my entire life to this state, to this nation, and to the land that we live on. I was acting governor of Nebraska back when it was only a territory. Not even a decade ago, I was in Washington, serving on President Cleveland's administration as Secretary of Agriculture. Ah, it wouldn't be worth our time for me to list all I have been and all I have done. But I will tell you my proudest achievement, and I know this would be of great interest to you, given your profession. Surely you have noticed this land is lush with trees. Not many years ago, this was far from the case. This land used to be barren, lifeless. Little more than grass and brush. But I and my family changed all of that. We turned this into a land of trees. Not only that, but we spread our mission far and wide with the founding of Arbor Day. You are no doubt familiar with that holiday?"

"Yes," Neville was relieved that he could be honest about that. "In fact," he hoped this next point would please Morton, "I was born on an Arbor Day."

His statement had the desired effect. Another gleam came to Morton's eyes and he cocked his head back. "Indeed? And what is your day of birth?"

"I was born April 10th."

The old man's eyes widened. "The year!"

"1872."

Morton gasped and shuffled excitedly in his bed until a jolt of pain stopped him. "Are you aware," he said as soon as the pain faded, "that you were born on the very first Arbor Day?"

"Truly?" This fact interested Neville far less than it did Morton, but it was best that he humor the man. At first, he'd thought the excitement had simply been the fact that his 29th birthday had recently passed.

Nodding, Morton clenched his thick hands together and stared thoughtfully at his blanketed feet. "Perhaps your being here is part of a divine plan."

"Truly?" Neville said again, realizing he'd said it with the exact same tone as before.

"I suppose," Morton turned his eyes back toward Neville, "it is past time I tell you why I paid your bail and brought you to my home." He leaned in and lowered his voice. "You saw it, too, didn't you?"

"What?" In his confused and intimidated state, Neville couldn't think what "it" might be.

"Please, do not play coy with me," Morton said, his teeth clenched in frustration. His eyes were wide and frenzied now, two grey orbs petrifying Neville like Medusa's gaze. "You saw the creature."

CHAPTER TWO

NEBRASKA CITY WAS never meant to be a long stop. He had only wanted the train station. There, with the little money he had left, he bought a ticket. After that, he purchased some food and drink in town. While waiting for the train, he developed a powerful urge to relieve himself. He found a tree, as any man had a right to do. As his waste trickled against the mighty trunk, he heard a high-pitched creaking sound in the branches above. It sounded like a grating giggle. His flow of warm relief dammed up, as he didn't like being watched.

"Go away," he snarled, thinking his watcher was a child, albeit one with a heavy ailment of the throat.

But the giggling continued, forcing him to glance up into the tree's dark green canopy. What Neville saw staring back down at him was no child. Not a child of God at least.

He saw little of the face except two large yellow eyes, larger than his mother's fine china. At first, his mind told him he was just seeing a large owl of some kind. Then he saw the rest of it. The body was small and sleek like a young child's, yet its limbs were long, stretching out like branches. It had no hands that Neville could see, but claws, long as knives. The abomination appeared to be covered in grass and sticks, the skin beneath a light green, and it had the foul odor of a beast from the fields.

Before Neville could comprehend the twisted shape lingering above him, the creature bellowed out another giggle, this one sounding less human and more rodent-like. Only then did Neville understand what this was—a grotesque, malevolent gnome.

He grabbed his axe, which had been resting against the trunk beside him. But as soon as the handle was in his grip, the gnome leapt from the tree, knocking Neville to the ground. The creature used all four of its limbs to propel it across the grass, toward town. Neville wasted not a second in scrambling to his feet, his blood racing with terror and fury, and chased after it.

By the time he realized the chase was futile, he was in the middle of town, swinging both his axe and his exposed member until he was tackled to the ground by several horrified citizens.

"A gnome, you say?"

Morton rested against the headboard, staring up at the ceiling thoughtfully, hands folded against his stomach. Outside, moonlight was beginning to shine through the bedroom windows.

"My word for it would be 'demon'," the old man said. "Regardless, your description indeed fits what I have encountered."

Neville's heart melted with relief at those words. To have what he had experienced be validated—and by this man, of all men—was almost enough to mend Neville's memory of that humiliation. Almost.

"Tell me, Mr. Gibbons," Morton said, leaning forward and again shifting those solemn but mighty eyes on Neville. "During the short time you've been in this house, have you heard scratching?"

Neville had to think about it, but then remembered the scratching from beneath the floors downstairs. He nodded.

"And what, do you think, is the cause of that noise?" The old man leaned in, close enough that Neville could smell his breath, stinking of damp, rotten vegetables. Neville didn't imagine his own breath smelled much better, but Morton didn't seem bothered.

"I don't know," Neville said. Morton's brows furrowed; he demanded an answer. "Mice?" Neville shrugged, uncertain what he was meant to say. "Rats?"

Morton chuckled. Apparently, this was the kind of answer he'd anticipated. "A disgusting thought, but reasonable. In truth, what you had heard were black-tailed prairie dogs."

"What?"

"Have you ever seen one?"

"No." Neville had heard of prairie dogs but had never cared to actually learn what one was. He pictured a large dog or maybe something akin to a coyote, crawling underneath the floor with its long black tail in tow.

"It's a type of rodent," Morton explained, immediately throwing Neville's imagery into the fire. "Think of a fat squirrel without the bushy tail. We used to see many out here, acres upon acres of land covered in their holes. You will not find as many out this way any longer. In the eastern part of the state, you can, but not here—at least not until recently."

Morton shifted and winced again. "The first time I encountered one was in the dining room a few months back. I'd mistaken it for a woodchuck. After that, more and more began to present themselves here and there. They would appear and we would dispatch them—if we could catch them—as one does with vermin. But their numbers only continued to grow, not shrink. Now, it seems there is an entire colony living beneath our feet."

"Truly?" Neville made a mental note to stop saying that.

"It seems impossible, doesn't it? For them to survive in such an environment?"

"It does." Though, in truth, Neville had no idea what was or wasn't possible for an animal he had only just learned about.

"Furthermore," Morton said, "you have no doubt noticed plants growing in certain places." Neville recalled the grass popping up near the dining room clock. "Not a plausible feat, is it? For such plants to not only grow but thrive in an environment with little fresh air or sunlight or water? And like with the prairie dogs, no matter how many times one is dispatched, they only come back in greater numbers. But the curiosity doesn't end there. Many other creatures have appeared in this house. Animals that haven't been seen around here for a long time. Strange birds, insects, snakes."

Neville shuddered at that last one. He didn't fear snakes, other than the fact that they reminded him of lizards, which he found repulsive. He hated their little legs.

"Once," Morton continued, "a prairie chicken was found defecating all over the kitchen." He scowled with revulsion. "Fortunately, Thomas killed it.

"You can see then that this house, my family's house, has gone to the devil. But it does not end there! Not only has this decay affected my home, but my body as well. It feels as though my entire physical being decided to fail me in an instant. And I have these . . . " He rolled the sleeve of his nightshirt up to his bicep to reveal red, flaking skin. The sight made Neville nauseous, and he was grateful when Morton quickly rolled the sleeve back. "My physician told me a rash of this sort might be caused by wild parsnip. Which, incidentally, is among the plants we've seen growing in the house. You understand my crisis then? This is supposed to be a home, a place of comfort and safety for my family. But my sons, Joy and Paul, and their families couldn't even stand to spend the summer here last year. This has been their summer home for years! And with the state of things having only grown worse these past months, I doubt they will even *attempt* coming back this year."

Morton paused, and Neville wondered if the old man wanted him to say something to that. But as soon as he tried to utter a syllable, Morton's barking voice interrupted. "My sons insist there must be a 'reasonable' explanation for this phenomenon. Not one of them believes me about the creature." A look of deep pain came over Morton's face. It was more than just the hurt of being doubted by his own flesh and blood, even Neville could see that.

"Four sons," Morton mumbled hazily. "I have four sons. Or I . . . Yes . . . "

Neville feared Morton would be trapped in this stupor, but the man managed to shake himself out of it. "Even Thomas," he continued. "Mr. Dailey believes as much, that there must only be 'reasonable' explanations. But there is no reason here. Only the creature."

Neville nodded as if he understood, but he didn't. The gnome? How could the gnome be responsible for Morton's illness and the prairie dogs and snakes and wild parsnips?

"Indeed," Morton said, agreeing with a statement Neville hadn't even made. "How has the creature perpetuated this curse? Where does its power come from? I do not know. But I know it is the perpetrator."

Neville thought back to earlier that day, chasing the gnome into town until it vanished seemingly into thin air. Perhaps such a creature did have great and terrible powers, including the power to curse others. A hot, panicked feeling flooded through his chest. Did this mean he was cursed as well?

"But why?" he asked, fighting a building dryness in his throat.

Morton shrugged. "I ask that question often. I've only ever strived to do the best for my family, for this country, indeed, for the whole world! I falter at times. I have made mistakes as any man is wont to do. But I surely haven't done anything so terrible as to deserve this violation of my home and person. But then, I suppose, such savages need no reason to commit beastly injustices."

Savage. Yes, that was the word for it. The heat in Neville's chest was no longer panic, but hatred. Hatred at the thought of that thing, that savage, trying to ruin the life of a good man.

"I thought I was alone," Morton continued, and for the first time that night, he gave a small smile. This unnerved Neville. There was something unbecoming about a smile on such a man's face. To his relief, the smile vanished, as if it had been little more than a muscle spasm. "Until today, when I heard of a strange man madly running about town, exposing himself . . . "

"That was not . . . " Neville tried to explain.

Morton raised his hand. "Please do not interrupt. As I was saying, I heard talk of this strange man, in the sheriff's custody, ranting and raving about a 'gnome'. His description fit the very creature who, gazing at me in the night, often visits my nightmares. A creature committed to destroying me, my family, my legacy. When I heard of this man, I felt, at long last, that I might have an ally. Was I correct?"

"Oh, yes," Neville said without hesitation. "Yes."

Morton's eyes lit up with pleasure, but his mouth remained mercifully downward. "How would you feel about staying here and working for me, Mr. Gibbons? Your job would be simple. Hunt the creature and kill it. We have guns and knives at your disposal, though it seems you already possess your weapon of choice."

Neville looked proudly upon Alexander's sharp blade.

"Now, this may not be the preferred work of a lumberjack. But it is a noble task."

Neville's heart fluttered. Never before had anyone deigned to seriously call him a lumberjack. Certainly, his father would never call him such a thing. Neville *truly* was a lumberjack. There could be no doubt about that now that a man like Julius Sterling Morton called him such. Not only that, but he was being recruited for a noble task: the triumph of civilization over savagery.

"I promise you'll be compensated fairly," Morton explained,

"and you can live here, in this house. There is a guest room downstairs. You'll be housed, fed, but you will also receive monetary payment once the deed is done. Shall we say 600 dollars? In the meantime, I will happily cover the costs of any supplies. I can fund other needs you may have—new clothes, for instance. You need not spend a penny of your own during your time here. How does that suit you?"

Neville's stomach churned with excitement, and there was a stir in his groin. He would be more than just a lumberjack. He would be a warrior. A knight. Sir Neville. If—*when*—he succeeded in his task, he would be famous the world over. Who wouldn't be talking about the dangerous, powerful creature that nearly destroyed a great man? Furthermore, who wouldn't be talking about the brave soul who conquered that creature? He imagined his father, at one of his dull dinner parties, forced to sit and listen to his crusty friends wax on and on about the American hero, Neville. His brothers, for all of their accomplishments, would be known as "Neville Gibbon's brother". Perhaps the poor sods could use that to their advantage. John could be elected pope by the very merit of being the brother of a legendary hero. As tribute to his mighty brother, John would call himself Pope Neville I. What a turn for the rotten boy who used to lock his younger brother in their mother's wardrobe for hours on end! Now the first American pope, only for his relation to that very brother. He pictured John in full papal regalia, kissing his feet. It was a shame that only old men became pope; it would be delicious for their father to live to see that.

"Mr. Gibbons?" Morton said, shaking Neville out of his silent daydream. "Do you accept my offer?"

"I do," Neville said, twisting Alexander's handle excitedly.

Morton's mouth twitched into another unsuitable smile, but Neville was too excited to be disturbed by it. The old man shifted and squirmed awkwardly out of his covers until his pale, veiny legs hung from the side of his bed. Apparently, Neville had, if only temporarily, reinvigorated him.

"Come," Morton said, snatching a cane resting beside his bed, "let me show you around Arbor Lodge."

CHAPTER THREE

The HOUSE, as Morton explained, was built in 1855. In its first iteration, it had been little more than a cabin, consisting only of four rooms. Many expansions had been made over the years, including the addition of the second floor in the '60s and another major remodeling in the '70s. Arbor Lodge had grown from a simple cabin into a mansion.

"Like a tree," Morton said proudly, "growing from a humble seedling."

In the upstairs hall, the door across from Morton's bedroom was closed. "That is Carrie's room," Morton explained mournfully. He pointed to a portrait hanging beside the bedroom depicting a poised and elegant woman in a dark dress. "Caroline, my wife. She passed many years ago. But I believe her presence is still here."

Neville said nothing, but he hoped that wasn't true. The woman in the portrait looked like she was about to reproach him. She reminded him of the strict tutor his parents forced on him when he was a child, Mrs. Garrison, an unpleasant woman looming over him with her switch at the ready. She would hit him with that rod of hickory, like the Roman soldier flogging Christ, and neither his father nor even his soft-hearted mother had done anything to stop her.

Caroline looked similar to Mrs. Garrison with those dark, stern features. Perhaps the image of Morton's late wife was slightly younger and prettier, but the haughty air was the same. No, he wanted nothing to do with that "presence". But he held his tongue. He was certain if he deigned to vocalize his thoughts to the wistful widower, their arrangement would be severed before it could begin. Even if he hadn't been in desperate need of the money and security, the warmth and acceptance emanating from Morton was too intoxicating. He wanted it to never fade. *Needed* it to never fade.

There were more rooms toward the back of the house, but Morton had little interest in showing them. He did take care to present the bathroom, which was beside his bedroom. The installation of indoor plumbing was one of the most exciting recent additions. Once the bathroom was sufficiently admired, Morton brought the tour downstairs and showed Neville the room he would be staying in, which was across from the parlor. The guest room was spacious and there was a row of windows that no doubt greatly lit the space in the daytime, but at the moment, the evening dimness and boggish wallpaper made it feel dark and constricted. There were shelves covered with books, also making the room feel smaller. The bed in the corner at least looked cozy and well-made, though it was coated in dust, like the rest of room.

"This had been the only bedroom when the frame house was built," Morton explained. "You no doubt know of James Denver?"

"Denver? I have been there, yes."

"No, no. Not the city, though it was named for him. I am referring to General James Denver."

He waited for a response from Neville. When he received none, he grumbled.

"Do young men learn *nothing* these days? General Denver was a true American hero. He stayed in this very room while negotiating the Table Creek Treaty with the Pawnee. A great win for the expansion of this country. I think the treaty served everyone quite fairly in the end. The United States has this exquisite land, and, from what I understand, the Pawnee have a nice little allotment in the territory south of Kansas. One can only hope they know what to do with it. Mr. Dailey is a Pawnee, you know. A decent enough fellow, isn't he? Civilized, at least for the most part, and I believe he has Denver to thank for that. Yes. Indeed, it was expert diplomacy on the General's part. And during that time, he stayed in this very room. A great man performing a noble deed. That is why you will be in here."

A great man. A true American hero. Neville had to temper his excited breathing so he wouldn't alarm Mr. Morton. A great man performing a noble deed had been here. Now, it was Neville's turn.

A silence settled between the two men, the faint sound of

scratching rising from beneath the floor. Morton scowled at the noise and motioned for Neville to follow him.

The next stop of the tour was the dining room. This time Neville could properly read the writing on the oval stained glass windows. "Small Cheer And Great Welcome Makes A Merry Feast" circled half the ovals. Beneath this phrase was the glasswork image of the tree with a banner wrapping its trunk reading "Arbor Lodge". Beneath that was another banner: "Virtutie Praemium".

"The Morton crest," Morton said, having followed Neville's eyes. "That quote is from Shakespeare, The Comedy of Errors."

Neville nodded. He'd been forced to read much Shakespeare throughout his life but was unfamiliar with that one.

"We've had many guests in this room," Morton reflected. He paused and eyed Neville disapprovingly. "Incidentally, our house has a rule you might be familiar with, regarding hats." Panicked, Neville quickly removed his hat as though it weren't too late. "It is no matter, just keep that in mind for the future."

Neville tightly gripped Alexander as Morton led him into the parlor. So humiliating. No doubt, the man now thought him a disrespectful pig. He wondered if he should apologize. He had simply forgotten the hat was on his head. That was all. Besides, he hadn't been in anybody's private home for at least two years; some manners were bound to be forgotten. Neville decided to say nothing.

Morton motioned to the parlor's piano, unmindful of the lumberjack's turmoil. "Carrie was an excellent piano player. She could light up the entire room with her music. I miss the sound."

Neville noticed what looked to be a long piece of grain poking from the floor beneath the instrument. Before he could comment, his attention was arrested by a massive painting covering the eastern wall. It was so breathtaking he even forgot the hat incident. It depicted a sweeping scene: a grassy field on a sunny day. On the left portion of the painting stood several men and women; they were white and well dressed, clean and civilized. Just looking at them filled Neville with pride. The men wore fine suits, the women in modest dresses. They stood nobly beneath the shade of a great tree. They were looking out at the group along the right side of the painting. These fellows Neville found to be less savory—a group of natives dancing in an open field. Neville could practically hear whatever horrendous drum beat they might have been dancing to.

Morton stood beside Neville, clutching the top of his cane, his mouth gaping in awe as if he were seeing this painting for the first time as well. "I commissioned this several years ago. It was done by a man named William Haskell Coffin. Very talented, wouldn't you say? What you are seeing here is the signing of the Table Creek Treaty." He pointed to the most prominently shown white man in the painting, a clean-shaven fellow standing firm and tall, a piece of paper in his hand. "That is General Denver." He next pointed to a woman in a yellow dress, not too far from where Denver stood. "That is Caroline. The man next to her," he pointed to another clean-shaven man standing profile as if posing for a coin, "that is me."

Impressed as Neville was, a more unassuming figure captured his attention. It was a man in a hat, sitting in the grass beside General Denver. His face couldn't be seen, as he was looking toward the dancing natives like the rest of his compatriots. Neville imagined that this figure was him. He was there with the rest of them, taming a wild land. His member stiffened at the thought, so prominently he placed his hat over his groin, lest Morton become privy to his shame.

"Gibbons," Morton said, half to himself. "That is an Irish name, is it not?" The tone in his voice wasn't disdainful, but it wasn't impressed either. Neville's swelling immediately began to deflate.

"My father's father was Irish," Neville said. There was no point in lying. "His mother's family was German."

"Indeed?"

"And I am German on my mother's side."

"A Teuton then." The old man smiled again. Neville wished Morton would stop doing that, but was relieved that he'd said the right thing. "Carrie was partially Irish as well. Perhaps I, too, have some cross pollination in my blood. It could certainly be worse." He motioned to the painting. "We, the Teutonic race, have a noble duty. We are the arbiters of civilization, peace, reason. It is not always a pleasant task, but it is of the utmost importance. The world would fall into ruin without us."

Neville's heart cried out with pride. Yes. The pursuit of civilization was the duty of the Teutonic race. Manifest Destiny. And he was a Teuton, a warrior tasked with bringing savagery to the axe, beating and cutting and chopping the wild until it was tamed, subservient to the whims of reason. It was not a pleasant task—though every thought of it excited him—but it had to be done.

Morton led Neville past a shelf full of fine china and books and directed his attention to four oval photographs on the wall. Each depicted one of Morton's sons. Neville felt deep resentment for all four of the young men. There was a snobbish arrogance in the way they posed for the camera, sniveling boys trying to look serious and graceful. They reminded Neville of his own brothers, or the boys he had to suffer in school and college. But what made him feel worse was the starry reverence Morton gave them, far superseding any that Neville himself received from the man. At the end of the day, they were Morton's sons, and Neville wasn't.

"Joy is my oldest. He lives in Chicago, quite the brilliant businessman. He owns a salt enterprise that he has very high hopes for." From Joy, he continued down the line from oldest to youngest, gushing about his sons Paul and Mark until he finally reached his youngest, Carl. The name was the only word he was able to utter before stopping. Neville thought the pause was to clear his throat, until the old man began to clutch his cane as if it were the only thing keeping him upright. His breathing grew heavy, and he uttered quietly pained groans.

"Mr. Morton?" A voice came from the dining room, so sudden it nearly made Neville drop his axe and hat. He turned to see Thomas Daily rushing in.

"I'm afraid I've over-exerted myself," Morton said, looking only at the floor. "Please escort me to bed, Mr. Dailey."

Hardly acknowledging Neville aside from stray glances, Thomas and Morton shuffled out of the parlor and up the stairs. Once alone, Neville turned his attention again to the incredible painting of the Table Creek Treaty signing. It gave him a powerful feeling that he had fallen into something great. He had no earthly idea what exactly that greatness was. Perhaps he didn't need to articulate it. All that mattered was that it was reaching out to him, and he was not going to waste a moment before grabbing its hand.

He shook with excitement. It was destiny. He would slay the gnome and tame this land once and for all. He would be loved, celebrated. He would be remembered.

But these lofty hopes immediately shattered when he caught a glimpse of Morton's fine china and saw the man staring back. This pitiable fellow was short and thin, with a perpetually hunched back, a scraggly black beard, and filthy clothes. He was not like those glorious Teutons in the painting. He was grotesque, pathetic. How could this being, who had been thrown out of three lumber camps for incompetence, possibly succeed at the great task before him?

Neville tore his eyes away, squeezing them tightly. Morton saw something in him, didn't he? He held onto that thought. Doubt was weakness. If he wanted to prove his true worthiness, this was his first test. He needed to kill the doubt. Slaughter it like the sickly, useless animal it was.

Beneath his feet came a chorus of scratching, the sound overwhelming the ticking of the dining room's grandfather clock. He opened his eyes to find a pair of tiny black eyes staring at him from across the room. The creature was on the sofa, standing alertly on its hind legs, long arms curved like a praying mantis. Its body was like a large, furry potato. It stood still. A prairie dog, he presumed. He raised his axe; this beast would be his first kill, a sacrifice representing all his doubt.

But before he could take a single step forward, the rodent cocked its head and vibrated its whole body as it gave a shrill, repetitive chirp. When he made a dash toward it, the little demon quickly retreated. By the time Neville reached the sofa, he saw nothing but a small, dark hole in the floor.

He dined alone on watery, tasteless soup and stale bread. Unappetizing as it was, it felt like a feast. He hadn't realized just how hungry he was until he began eating.

Once his bowl and plate were clean, he went outside to sit on the front porch and look out at the trees. They reached proudly toward the moonlight which illuminated their leaves. A dazzling arrogance. Neville wanted to cut every last one of them down. Unfortunately, he knew Morton wouldn't approve. In fact, the man would be mortified. Neville pressed Alexander dutifully against his lap. It was best to resist this lustful urge.

He heard the house's front door open and close behind him and glanced to see the looming figure of Thomas Dailey.

"I'm going to retire for the night," Thomas said. "I have a cabin on the grounds, not too far from here. Please hesitate to bother me unless it's serious."

Neville said nothing. As he looked at Thomas, he thought back to the scene in the William Haskel Coffin painting: natives dancing in that wild, frightening manner he'd read about in books throughout his life. Yet, Neville found it hard to imagine Thomas being so frightening. If anything, the man was rather dull.

Thomas held his nose, even in the crisp night air. Neville's stench must have been too much for him.

"Mr. Morton is all right," the driver continued with a now nasally voice. "Or at least as good as he can be. Carl, his youngest son, died in January. Mr. Morton likes to pretend it's been more than four months, and that it's not still ripping him apart."

"I see," Neville said. He suppressed the twinge of pleasure at this news. How satisfying that one of those arrogant boys was rotting in the ground! How grand this was. Morton had a youngest son-shaped hole in his heart, and now Neville, also the youngest of four boys, was here.

"So, you're a lumberjack?" Thomas stepped down from the porch. He released his nose; more space seemed to negate the smell a bit.

"Yes," Neville said, tickled. Yes, he was a lumberjack. Now that Morton had said it, it was the truth. Morton had brought it into being.

Thomas looked Neville up and down. "You certainly have the appearance of one," he said. The skepticism in his voice dissipated Neville's pleasure. "But your face, your skin, it's soft. I don't have to feel it, I can tell. There's a look about you. You strike me as the kind of fellow who might be *running* a lumber company, not working for one."

Thomas dared to call his skin soft? Neville leapt to his feet, axe at the ready.

Thomas raised his hands and backed away. "Hey," he said, shrinking himself, "no need for that. I didn't mean anything by it."

The look of fear in Thomas' long face was enough to sate Neville's anger. At least, he was satisfied enough to lower Alexander. But he needed to say more, to put Thomas in his place.

"I wouldn't expect you to understand the undertaking I have

been given." He spoke to the driver like a priest lecturing a petulant child. "In fact, if I were you, I wouldn't bother putting my brain through such strain."

Thomas clenched his teeth.

"Your undertaking," Thomas said, "is to kill the creature?"

Neville nodded, irritated by the undertone of skepticism.

"You know," Thomas continued at a slow, cautious pace, "Morton is a confused man. I don't doubt he's seen things. Children from town play in these woods all the time. Not to mention the animals. But the creature? The curse? It's all make-believe. His health is failing. His son is dead. His beloved Arbor Lodge is falling apart. He still hasn't recovered from the loss of his wife. I think he's just trying to find something to blame for all of that. I don't know what you're trying to achieve, but you're just confusing him more."

This gave Neville a surge of anger, nearly inspiring him to raise his weapon again. But he was able to restrain this, reminding himself that Thomas wouldn't, couldn't understand. "Only a Teuton could comprehend the nuances of this situation," he explained, trying to make his tone as acrid as his skin. "I wouldn't expect a savage to understand. Stick to what you know best and leave this to me."

Thomas grunted and looked at his feet. For some inexplicable reason, he seemed less angered at this and more disappointed.

"Your first job tomorrow will be to go into town and buy yourself some new clothes." Thomas spoke mechanically, repeating the instructions Morton had told him to pass on. "We'll of course provide you the money. Then, for god's sake, take a bath and wash these clothes."

"Wash my clothes?" Neville was flummoxed. "That's a woman's task!"

"Have you seen any women around here?" Thomas snapped back. "It's just you, the old man and myself. You don't need a woman to wash your clothes. You have hands, don't you? Surely, you don't want *me* to do it, soil your Teutonic garments with my . . . " He bit his tongue. "I'm already doing nearly everything else around here. All you have to worry about is your 'hunt'."

Neville sat back down, quietly pouting and holding his axe to his chest.

Thomas looked satisfied. That was that. But, despite this, he had one last thing to say. "Listen, curse or not, this isn't a healthy place. I would suggest you head back home or wherever you were going."

When the only response the lumberjack gave was a hateful glare, Thomas shrugged and walked off toward the woods where his cabin was. He relied on the stars and the moon for light, not yet turning on his lantern. Maybe he worried Neville wanted to chase after him.

But Neville didn't move. He pouted on the porch, still flustered that he would have to wash his own clothes. He didn't even know *how* to wash clothes. The frustration became too much, and he again jumped to his feet. He had an overwhelming desire to feel Alexander's blade dig into something. He scanned the dark woods and picked the nearest tree. It had a thick trunk and a dense, low bushel of branches. Even in the darkness, the leaves appeared densely green.

Before he had a moment to think, Neville charged at the tree and, with a mighty cry, cut into the trunk. He chopped again and again. Only once Alexander's blade was deep in the wood, did Neville realize what he had just done. Panicked, he tried to pull the axe out, but it wouldn't budge. He tugged harder and, when Alexander finally did let go, the force threw Neville to the ground, knocking the breath out of him.

When he recovered, he was relieved to find the tree still standing. At the same time, a deeper part of him was unsatisfied, wanted to see the tree fall. But he let his calmer side win the day. In the moon's glow, he could see the nasty gash in the tree's trunk that the axe had left. Panicked, his first thought was to fill the scar with mud. But the idea was foolish. All he could do was hope that nobody would notice, especially not Mr. Morton.

Beneath the singing of crickets, he heard a distant giggle. Somehow his eyes knew exactly where to look. From the top of the house, along that massive roof, two large yellow eyes peered back at him. They didn't blink or shift, they only stared, seemingly expressionless. Yet he could tell the one those eyes belonged to was amused. Readying Alexander, he hurtled forward, stumbling several times and nearly falling along the way, his only thought to get to the roof. He tried to climb from the outside of the house but couldn't get decent footing anywhere. He would have to find a way from the inside. But when he barged through the front door and reached the top of the stairs, he paused, not knowing where to go next.

"Neville?" The voice was Morton's, bellowing from behind his bedroom door. "Go to bed."

After some hesitation, Neville lowered the axe. Yes, that seemed like a good next move. It had been a long, strange day, and he needed his rest. He had a feeling that, even if he did reach the roof, the gnome would be gone. The fighting would have to wait. The gnome wouldn't die tonight.

But it *would* die.

Thomas Dailey returned to his cabin without any trouble. He plopped onto his cot, sighing in relief. What a day it had been. With another sigh he pulled out his corncob pipe, lit it up and sucked in the sweet tobacco while listening to the crickets outside. A deep calm settled over him. Some days, it felt like moments like these were the only thing that made it all worth it.

Goddamn did he hate it here. Maybe it would be better to leave. Go somewhere else. Maybe his uncle down in Oklahoma was at least still alive.

But no. He had a good thing here. Painful as it was to have to care for that old man, to have to do the work of several people but only paid as well as one; to be coachman, butler, groundskeeper, and cook for a house that was falling apart; to have to put up with Mr. Morton's grumblings; to see that disgusting painting in the parlor every day. Painful as it all was, he was fortunate. He had money, food, and even though this little cabin was a shithole, it was better than having to live in the house with Morton. Most people back home would beg to be in the position he was in. Maybe.

He sucked in the tobacco even more deeply. That Neville. Damn it, that Neville. From the very beginning, he had a feeling Morton's unexpected guest would be trouble. There had been a brief moment where he hoped, perhaps naively, that there might be more to Neville. But as soon as the man started rambling about "savages" and "Teutons", Thomas finally understood why Mr.

Morton took to him. Just another racist white man, a dime a dozen and then some, with hardly the brain to think for himself.

Yet it wasn't that simple either. There *was* something more, something that made Thomas' gut squirm. Why that strange, scrawny little man scared him so much, he couldn't say. But he had a feeling something terrible was going to happen. It was probably nothing. Still, he'd had that same feeling when he was a kid, hadn't he? Right before the government came and dragged him off to the school.

Maybe there was something to this feeling then. Maybe he needed to leave. Go find a nice woman. Though frankly, he'd prefer a man: a big, hairy, barrel-chested fellow with a throbbing dick, using Thomas in whatever way he wanted. He had to stop himself from chewing excitedly into the stem of his pipe at this thought. Thomas would have to, of course, settle for a woman or nothing at all. Otherwise, it would be a sin, wouldn't it? At any rate, he wasn't one to scoff at a supple pair of breasts. Maybe he and his wife could have a nice home and some children, and they could take in a handsome, barrel-chested boarder or two. It would be grand, and all he had to do first was leave Nebraska City.

Somewhere in the distance, he heard the whooping of coyotes. The tricksters. He didn't remember much about being Pawnee anymore, but he could at least recall some stories. Somewhat. The whooping grew louder before ceasing altogether.

Mischief really was afoot.

He wasn't going to leave. He knew that. Really, where would he go? Oklahoma, perhaps. Back to Kansas City? To Omaha? Return to a life of swindling and ripping people off so he could afford a night's meal?

No matter where he went, no matter what he did, bad feelings were going to chase him. That was his lot in life. But as far as he could tell, listening to bad feelings wouldn't feed him, wouldn't shelter him, wouldn't make him money. He'd just have to stick with it for as long as he could. Besides, it was only a matter of time before Mr. Morton grew bored of this newfound curiosity. But Thomas supposed he'd do well to watch his mouth before then.

And, who could say? Maybe it would all be fine in the end.

CHAPTER FOUR

NEVILLE WOKE UP that morning feeling more rested than he had in years. He'd dreamt he was towering and powerful, and finishing off the tree he had cut into with Alexander the night before. Each chop sent waves of shuddering pleasure through his body. He chopped and chopped, moaning with delight after each strike. Faster, faster. His heart contracted. He couldn't stop, he was coming so close, so close. Then, with one last thunderous burst, the tree fell. Hot sticky sap erupted from its stump, covering Neville's tan and chiseled body. His satisfied body twitching, he mounted the stump, allowing the geyser of sap to shoot up into and around his body.

"Manifest Destiny," he had muttered before awakening, finding most of his body to be free of sticky goo, aside from his legs.

Shortly after cleaning the mess, Neville joined Mr. Morton for breakfast. They ate on the front porch of the house. The morning air was cool, and the birds sang.

"Look at them," Morton said, gaping at the trees as if seeing them for the first time. "It wasn't many years ago, this land was barren and lifeless." The old man turned his eyes to Neville. The intensity of the gaze made Neville squeeze Alexander's handle between his thighs. "As a lumberjack, surely your knowledge of trees must be exceptional."

Neville's thighs clenched harder. He didn't like where this was going.

"Tell me," Morton said, pointing to what looked like a very tall Christmas tree. "What type of tree is that?"

Neville searched through his cloudy mind for some kind of guess. All he could think was "Christmas tree" but he knew that would be an idiotic answer.

Quickly losing patience, Morton answered for him. "Norway Spruce."

He pointed to another tree, arching his eyebrows in anticipation of an answer. The tree was tall and thin with few branches. It only had small wisps of greenery toward the top. Again, Neville scrambled through his mind, but couldn't even find a foolish answer.

"Corsican Pine," Morton said. He added reproachfully: "These are easy ones my boy."

Neville went cold with shame. He couldn't identify any of these trees. He didn't even know the names of any trees besides perhaps Maple. Furthermore, he had no interest in knowing what they were called. He didn't care to know anything about them except how it would feel to cut them down.

Morton pointed to another tree, and this time barely waited before answering. "Black Walnut."

The old man scanned the woods before finally pointing to another tree, which looked very familiar. "Surely, you know that one?"

Neville immediately recognized it as the tree he had chopped into the night before and had an urge to spew his breakfast onto the table. Did Morton somehow know what he'd done?

"Come on man," Morton barked, "you must know!"

Neville shook his head. If Morton had found him out, then denial was not a wise path. But he took it anyway.

Morton leaned back and sighed. "It is a bur oak." As he gazed at the tree, his disappointment gave way to reverence. "My favorite."

Neville sighed, too, satisfied that Morton didn't know what he'd done. But he also lamented this terrible start. No doubt Morton felt Neville was failing him. It would turn around. It would have to.

Then he was struck by inspiration. If naming trees was a battlefield where he would lose, then he'd turn attention to the battlefield where he wouldn't. The gnome.

"I think I will place traps around the grounds, with your permission. I will particularly focus on where the creature has been seen."

"Yes," Morton said. To Neville's frustration, the old man's loving focus was still on the tree.

"I can purchase them when I go into town."

Finally peeling his eyes from the tree, Morton frowned at Neville. "Do be careful. The creature is clever. Shall I have Thomas drive you into town?"

"No, I can walk."

"Fine. Do not forget to purchase new clothes. Perhaps while you are there, you can also pick up some provisions?"

Neville wanted to protest. He wasn't an errand boy, but he wouldn't argue with Mr. Morton either, so he pursed his lips and nodded.

It was not a friendly town. On the streets, in the shops, people frowned and glowered at him. Some appeared revolted by him, others seemed anxious; the worst were those who looked at him with suppressed amusement. He wanted to chop them all to pieces.

At least his venture had been fruitful. He was able to purchase two new shirts, and new pairs of undergarments, pajamas, pants, and socks. There seemed to be no bear traps in stock anywhere in town. He would have to speak to Mr. Morton about putting in an order to be shipped from elsewhere. Twenty seemed a good start, maybe thirty. In the meantime, he supposed he could make his own traps: pits and snares. Perhaps Mr. Dailey would have the primitive know-how to help with that task.

His last begrudging stop was the grocery store where he was to pick up sugar, salt, coffee, and butter. The store was run by a burly man who looked to be built like a lumberjack, but had sadly filled out from his wasted years as a grocer. His wife also helped run the store. A lean, pretty woman, but Neville resented her mean black eyes. Three boys galloped around the store, pretending they were riding through some battlefield, wooden sticks for guns.

"Come on Rough Riders!" their leader continuously cried. This was apparently the grocer's son.

"William!" one or both of his parents would shout whenever the boys made too much commotion. Neville wondered why they didn't make more of an effort to discipline their son. The imp looked old enough to help around the store, but instead was running about like a fool with his friends. Several times they nearly tripped Neville. Nothing would have been more satisfying than to see the rotten little smirk get beaten off of him.

"Haven't seen you before," the burly grocer said congenially as Neville paid for his provisions. His mean-eyed wife whispered in his ear and the man's friendly tone shifted. "Oh, so you're the fellow from yesterday."

Neville grew sick with anger, squeezing Alexander in one hand and his sack of clothes in the other. So that explained the mean, jeering, and disgusted looks he'd been getting from townspeople.

"I hear Mr. Morton has you in his employ," said the woman. Her voice was kinder than her eyes, but Neville knew she judged him. He felt it in her tone.

"Yes," Neville said.

"I wonder what he's got planned," muttered the burly man.

"All his other help left, so he took what he could get." The wife said this with no regard for Neville's presence.

"His task for me is of the utmost importance," Neville said, keeping his voice steady. "I would not concern yourselves with it." He put on the most condescending smile he could. They needed to know that his undertaking with Morton was far above them and their little lives.

The woman scoffed, and her husband looked perplexed. These reactions satisfied the lumberjack.

"Bang!" William shouted, his stick pointed at Neville, his crooked lips grinning deviously. "You're dead, Spaniard."

"William!" his mother hissed. The three boys galloped off to the back of the store, cackling.

"Can we please hurry this along?" Neville said through his teeth. "Mr. Morton cannot be kept waiting."

The couple said nothing more to him as they bagged his provisions. He could feel the disdain simmering from their souls. But it didn't matter what these simple people thought. It didn't matter what those little goblins, sniping at Neville from across the store as he left, thought either. All that mattered was Morton. As long as he needed Neville, the town's hands were tied. As long as J. Sterling Morton needed Neville, their resentment meant nothing.

Upon returning to the house, he noticed more patches of brown and green grass in the parlor, shooting up in various places. The scratching of the prairie dogs was also particularly loud, sounding almost as if they were hard at work on something.

After putting away the groceries, he went upstairs to the bathroom to bathe himself. Other than the scratching downstairs, the whole house was quiet. Morton was apparently either sleeping or had been well enough to go into town for business.

After his bath and a small lunch, Neville returned to his room, that room where General Denver had spent many nights, thinking of how to consort with the Pawnee, and he put on his new clothes. It was certainly a satisfying feeling, his skin and hair fresher than they had been in months. He placed his old dirty clothes in the wardrobe. He refused to wash them today, not unless Mr. Morton ordered him to.

A framed photograph above the nightstand caught his eye. It was of former President Cleveland and his administration, including one with Julius Sterling Morton. Here were all men, confident and noble—presumably all Teutons. The photograph brought back those feelings from childhood, learning about knights and lumberjacks and kings and other great men. His Uncle Neville, with whom he shared a family name, used to tell these stories. Neville's mother allowed these flights of fancy for it had given her beloved brother so much joy to regale his nephew. Neville's father, of course, resented it, but he couldn't control the older Neville.

In league with a key member of the Cleveland administration; it excited Neville to think of what his father, a rabid Harrison supporter in the election of '92, would think of this. How furious he would be! How aghast and offended . . .

At the same time, he shuddered at the very idea of his enraged father being in this room. It was a shameful fear. How strange to be on the eve of thirty and still so frightened of his father. But the man had always been a shadow over him. While his loving uncle used to encourage his fascination in lumberjacks, even buying him Alexander on his seventeenth birthday, his father did everything he could to snuff that interest out. Lumberjacks, he would explain in his instructor-like manner, were not heroes nor conquerors. They were just working men like any other. Perhaps it required some physical strength, but not much more than working in a steel factory or a field or even a chain gang.

"Are criminals heroes as well?" Neville could remember him barking.

No, such a profession was below a Gibbons. Neville would not humiliate his family by pursuing such dreams. For some time, Neville had resigned himself to his fate. He had gone to college to study history, intending to pursue a career path similar to his father's. After graduating with barely passing grades, a fact for which his father refused to celebrate his graduation, he spent years working under the man's thumb at the museum. The most abled years of his life, gone in a blink as he led a dull, mundane existence. He was even married for a year, at his parent's behest—an unremarkable woman named Claudia, some distant cousin of his. The slight, sickly woman had thankfully contracted tuberculosis and died, the happiest thing she had ever done for him. He supposed he couldn't blame her for the fact that she had been nothing to him. She could not possibly have fulfilled his truest desires. No person could. When Uncle Neville had died, a death that had actually upset him, he had been inspired to free himself from the mundanity. He gathered his money and fled to San Francisco to become a lumberjack.

Now he was here, hunting a creature he never before imagined existed. He was proud of where he was. A man with a true, noble purpose. He was overjoyed that his father wasn't here, indeed likely didn't even *know* Neville was here.

He sat on the bed and studied the picture of Morton, President Cleveland, and the rest of the administration. He imagined these men sitting together in Morton's parlor, smoking pipes and drinking brandy or something of the sort. Morton would entertain his old colleagues with the story of Neville, the man who had slain the monstrous gnome. Not only a brave warrior, but a fine lumberjack. Neville wouldn't be there with them; he would be somewhere else in the world, bringing an entire forest down by himself. Yet, through their fawning and admiration, he would be very present.

"That is indeed a man," President Cleveland would say. "I think I would have liked to have had a son like Neville."

The other administrators would murmur their agreement.

"Is he not too young to adopt?" one would jest. Yet none would laugh, as they would find the notion of calling Neville their son actually quite appealing.

"Ah, now there's an idea," Cleveland would say. "But surely the privilege could only possibly go to a man of presidential stature?"

Other men would chime in, arguing for their worthiness of adopting Neville, and the parlor would erupt in light, yet heated, argumentation.

Finally, Morton would speak up, silencing the rest. "I can assure you that I would like the privilege above all else. Furthermore, I would challenge each of you to a gentlemen's duel to decide the matter once and for all—yes, even you Mr. President."

Cleveland would chortle at this. "Well, I suppose I'm beat."

The room would be enlivened by gentlemanly laughter.

Neville quivered with excitement at the fantasy. Perhaps Morton *was* the person who could fulfill his truest desires.

His fanciful spell was suddenly broken when upstairs he heard a loud cry and a thud.

CHAPTER FIVE

HE RUSHED UP to Morton's bedroom to find the old man lying on the floor, curled up against the bearskin rug. He looked up at Neville with the ashen face of a man who had seen death and pointed to his desk, where he had apparently been sitting. Beneath the desk, a faint rattling could be heard. Then Neville saw the brown coiled body, its broad head raised, black tongue flickering.

"For god's sake," Morton pleaded, "kill the damn thing!"

But Neville was paralyzed. He knew what a rattlesnake bite could do, and this one was more than ready to strike.

"Kill it!" Morton shouted, a command more than a request.

Propelled by this order, the lumberjack took a meager step forward, Alexander at the ready. The snake raised its vibrating tail, its small eyes clearly on Neville. He stepped a little closer and stretched his axe outward, keeping his hands toward the bottom of the handle. He hoped he could kill it from this distance. Unfortunately, as he brought the axe down, it was immediately evident that Alexander's blade fell short. The snake didn't move, it wasn't even intimidated by these efforts. Neville let out an involuntary groan, any step closer would be too close. For whatever reason, he remembered that the ancient conqueror for whom his axe was named had died of poisoning. The thought was deeply disconcerting.

"Hurry up, man!" Morton barked.

The snake took the offensive, lunging forward with a piercing hiss. Neville yelped and tumbled backward, falling on top of his employer.

"Get off me!" Morton shouted, beating against Neville's shoulders. But Neville couldn't move, despite the old man's furious protestations. His legs felt like they were filled with molasses and nothing else.

The room was suddenly filled by another presence. This new entity snatched Alexander from Neville's hands.

"No!" the lumberjack screamed.

The molasses spread through his entire body, making him feeble and limp. Morton was finally able to use his limited strength to push the younger man off him.

Neville lay on the floor, curled like a child in the womb, with his eyes squeezed shut. He heard the snake hiss again, heard its angry rattle, before it was silenced by a loud thump.

The room became quiet, other than Morton's little clock, ticking apathetically. Neville opened his eyes to see Thomas standing over him. The man held Alexander in one hand, the tip of its blade reddened with blood, and the headless body of the rattlesnake in the other. Seeing his axe gave Neville some newfound strength, and he, as the rattlesnake once had, lunged forward and snatched it out of Thomas' hand. His weapon secured, he made a mad dash out of the room, down the stairs, out of the house and down the road. He only stopped when he realized he didn't know where he was running to, nor what he was running from.

His knee shook uncontrollably, bouncing Alexander like a newborn babe. He'd wiped the rattlesnake's blood off of the blade, but now it mockingly coated his sleeve. He sat on the front porch of the house, staring down at the label printed on the axe's handle. "Helko Werk". A German axe. A Teutonic axe. How unworthy he was of it. Over and over, he relived what had just occurred. Each time, he felt more humiliated. He had been so cowardly, so foolish. No doubt Mr. Morton thought nothing of him now.

Soon, he would be relinquished from his duties.

And then, he thought, *I will slit my throat.*

He hated himself, hated Thomas, hated the snake. Such a cruel test that had been. If only he'd had preparation. But a true man didn't need preparation.

Thomas stepped out of the house, holding the headless snake like a belt.

"Mr. Morton's okay," he said. "He's napping now."

Neville squeezed his axe, refusing to look up at the man.

Thomas sighed.

He knew he had to make amends. He didn't want to talk to Neville any more than the man wanted to talk to him. But from what Mr. Morton had told him before going to bed, Mr. Gibbons was still here to stay.

"He'll have some work to do," the old man had said, "if he wants to capture the gnome."

"So, you'll keep him here?" Thomas asked, feeling any air of hope inside himself whistle away. He had felt sure that the lumberjack was fired.

"You disapprove, Mr. Dailey?"

"Well," Thomas said, ignoring the amused condescension in Morton's voice, "he couldn't even kill a snake."

"Yes," Morton conceded, "it was a pitiful display. If he doesn't show any improvement, I suppose I will have to end this partnership of ours. But I cannot afford to let Neville go just yet, Mr. Dailey. He believes me."

If Neville was here to stay, Thomas would have to make some sort of peace, especially if he wanted his ominous feelings to come to nothing. He'd spent so much of his life sleeping with one eye open, he didn't want to go back to that now.

"I'm sorry for taking your axe," Thomas said. "But when I saw the snake, it seemed like the only thing that would do the trick."

"I could have handled it," Neville said.

Neither man believed this. In fact, Thomas had an urge to make some kind of joke about it. But for the sake of peace, he only nodded.

"You're probably right," he said, taking great pains to make sure there was no sarcastic undertone.

The quaking of the lumberjack's knees was now just a quiver, but he still looked sick. His eyes were closed tightly. Thomas wondered if this was adrenaline from the attack. Of course, he knew that humiliation could be worse than a thousand rattlesnake bites.

"Say," Thomas began. He paused with hesitation, wondering if he should continue. What the hell, he decided. "You look like you could use a drink. I've got some good whiskey in my cabin." Having a vile person to drink with was better than drinking alone.

He regretted making the offer immediately. Even in the interest of making peace, this was going too far. Neville wasn't the kind of man he wanted to be friends with, and he knew the feeling was mutual. Still, he hadn't had a nice drink or someone to drink with in a long, long time. Maybe, too, he was a little lonely.

"Am I going to be fired?" Neville asked, like a pitiful child.

"No," Thomas said. He didn't have a hint of doubt, but could tell his answer gave the small man little comfort. His eyes were locked on his axe's handle as if its "Helko Werk" label was a fascinating read.

"Only drunks and degenerates drink at this time," Neville muttered.

"Well—"

"Fine."

Thomas nodded, partly glad for the company but also wishing he'd had a chance to rescind his offer.

Thomas's cabin was spartan, just the way he liked it. No clutter or decorations: just a cot, a wooden chair, the chest containing his belongings, a small shelf, and the pungent smell of tobacco. The shelf contained only four items: a half-empty bottle of dark whisky and three filthy old glasses. He pulled down the bottle and two of the glasses.

It was only supposed to be one drink. But one became two and two became three. At first, neither man had any interest in speaking to the other; but the whisky flowed, and before long, they were talking and laughing bawdily. Thomas told funny stories of the mischief he and his friends would get up to when he was a child, back before he was taken to that horrible school. He also shared filthy jokes, ones he'd thought had been long beaten out of him. It brought him a great feeling of joy to have them bubbling to the surface again, so unexpectedly. It was like a part of him that he'd thought had long died was peeking in to say hello. Perhaps, if he thought hard enough about it, he'd be able to remember a few phrases of his native language as well.

Neville didn't say as much. But he laughed a surprising amount. Maybe Thomas was funnier than he realized. Or perhaps the whisky was better than he realized.

But when the liquor began to trickle away, so did the laughter and the jokes. It seemed Thomas had exhausted all his latent memories and for some reason, this made him deeply bitter.

Neville also seemed to grow bitter in the dense silence. His eyes darkened and his face sank into a scowl.

"I could have killed that snake," he said. His eyes suddenly stabbed into Thomas, a hot, resentful look.

"I'm sure," Thomas said hazily, still feebly trying to remove his mental blockage. He couldn't even recall the jokes he had been telling only minutes ago. It was as if he had only been visited by the *spirits* of those memories. Whispers of what once had been there in abundance—like those prairie dogs or all those plants— but had been chased away. Coming back to make sure you don't forget them. But they would be forgotten all the same, wouldn't they?

"I had it under control." Neville pointed a tiny finger at Thomas. "Next time, stay out of my goddamn way."

Thomas twitched as he suppressed a scoff. He still felt uncomfortable about antagonizing this man, especially with that damn axe lying on his lap.

"I am going to kill the bastard," Neville mumbled. "I am going to cut him to pieces."

"What?" A flash of terror tightened Thomas' face. "Oh, your creature."

Neville nodded. Flecks of whisky flew off his beard like water from a wet dog.

"Why do you think it's here?" Thomas asked.

"What?"

"Where does this creature come from? Why do you think it's here, of all places?"

Neville stuttered for a bit, trying to find the words until finally settling on something adequate. "It wants to destroy civilization."

A deep, cold laugh shot out of Thomas. "Civilization, huh?"

"Yes!" Suddenly, words were pouring out of Neville like a flood. "People think the war between civilization and savagery is won, that this world has been completely tamed. Not so. Yes, it is only a matter of time before the untamed parts see their reckoning. But there must be vigilance. The savages are howling at our gates . . . "

"Savages like me?" Thomas took a swig straight from the bottle, emptying it once and for all.

Neville stopped talking, unsure how to answer that while in the belly of the beast. This silence came as a pleasant surprise to Thomas. He had expected Neville's anger to escalate.

The wise thing to do would be to let this conversation fade away. See Neville back to the house, maybe do a little outside work to sweat off the drunkenness. But—and it was definitely the whisky's fault—he wasn't done yet.

"So," he continued, "this creature is trying to destroy civilization by making a prairie grow in Morton's house?"

Neville nodded.

"I don't understand the tactic."

"Morton is a champion of civilization," Neville said. "He brought trees to this land, he helped bring commerce, law. The gnome brought this curse to ruin him for what he represents."

"Or maybe your gnome just liked things the way they were before all the big cities and the big trees. But, you know, my people never had stories about such a creature. So maybe *you* all brought it here."

"I brought it?" Neville grunted. "How? Don't be ridiculous."

"Or maybe," he leaned in as if telling a ghost story, "the gnome was created by the land itself. Retribution for what white men did to it."

"What white men did to it . . . " Neville rose and immediately fell back onto the chair, trying to blink the dizziness out of his eyes.

"Well, whatever this creature is, I wish you happy hunting."

Their visit ended the way it had begun, in silence, neither man saying anything to the other.

CHAPTER SIX

BREAKFAST WAS HELD on the front porch again. Apparently, it had rained the night before, as the grass and air were moist and small puddles pocked the road.

Neville's head pounded something fierce. The whisky had mostly tapered off by bedtime, but obviously enough had remained to punish him come the morning. On top of that he'd slept poorly. Throughout the night, he kept hearing noises coming from the room above him—Caroline's room. The noises didn't sound human—more like someone was keeping a cow up there; the sound of dense hooves thudding against the floor, though the thuds were inconsistent, fading in and out. There was also an occasional growling sound, throaty and guttural. Frankly, the noises would have been manageable. It was the strong bovine stink wafting down into his room that kept him awake the most.

He had to suppress the memory of that smell to keep from vomiting his breakfast all over Mr. Morton. He couldn't imagine doing anything worse. The old man was congenial toward Neville this morning, as if the embarrassment from the night before was far from his mind. He spent most of the meal reminiscing about Caroline and how they had built a home and family together on this land. He recalled these memories with both tremendous joy and agony.

"Carrie has been gone for nearly twenty years. But I can still vividly remember the day we laid her to rest." His sad eyes were on Neville, but they also seemed to be looking somewhere very far off. "My love since boyhood. I've never truly acclimated to life without her. Have you ever been in love?"

Neville shook his head. It was a moronic question, unworthy of a man of Morton's standing. But he said nothing.

"It is a beautiful thing to have, but terrible to lose. Of all the things I've been, a widower is the most taxing."

"Indeed?" Neville realized that he was technically a widower, too. He would not share this fact with Morton, for then the old man would expect Neville to understand his pain. But when Neville thought about the late Claudia, her sallow and pathetic pale face, he couldn't conjure any grief. If anything, he just felt relieved. It had been a worthless little marriage, and she'd been miserable, too. But both of their parents had worried that if they didn't marry each other, they would marry no one. Claudia's death had freed them both. Had she lived, or God forbid had they any children, Neville would never have been able to flee San Francisco and pursue his dreams. It would have been more difficult, at least.

Perhaps tired of grief, Morton shifted the conversation to trees. He pointed out the various trees before them, rehearsing their taxonomies and function from rote. Neville didn't care. His only joy was in imagining the feeling of each tree falling at the mercy of Alexander's might. Morton's attention turned to his beloved bur oak, the one tree that had really been hit by Neville's axe, and suddenly went pale, his small mouth gaping. Without excusing himself, he quickly stood up and paced into the house.

Neville also paled. Had the old man somehow seen the mark he'd made? But when he looked at the tree, he couldn't see the gash. He sat and stared, puzzled at what could have bothered Morton, until he finally saw. Among the tree's bright green leaves were patches of brown. Decay. And it appeared it was only going to spread.

The sun sank across the sky as Neville spent his day patrolling the grounds, particularly focusing on the places the gnome had been spotted by Morton. His mind was running like a steam engine. He planned, strategized, thought of new plans and strategies when his initial ones no longer made sense, and then scrapped those as well. Every time his mind started to doubt that he knew what he was doing, he had to reaffirm that he in fact did. Morton had stated he was putting in an order for bear traps, that was a good start.

By the day's end, he had one morsel of success to savor. He'd caught a raccoon snooping around the carriage house. It had been quite the chase. The creature had nearly outrun him, but he'd managed to corner it at the back of the house. It took him a few strikes to get the miserable thing to quit moving, and by then it was a mess of blood and giblets. He himself became covered in blood, particularly in the process of disposing of the body. He still refused to wash his clothes, so he tucked this bloodied set away in the wardrobe, next to the clothes he had arrived with. He would, however, bathe himself.

The water was hot and steaming; a pleasant, purifying reward. His mind reeled excitedly with the fresh memory of the frightened raccoon, chittering and trembling as he decided its fate. Soon, the gnome would be in this same position. No longer would it utter that cruel, mocking giggle; instead, it would be whimpering for mercy. He would not turn it into paste like he had the raccoon for only one reason: Mr. Morton needed his trophy. The gnome's ugly head would do. Once this trophy was delivered, Morton would shower Neville with praise and respect and money and affection. Neville would transcend into legend; he would be remembered for all time.

His body swelled with rapture. Particularly one part of him swelled to a point where it could no longer be ignored. After pleasuring himself, he stepped out of the bath and used it to wash the raccoon blood from Alexander's blade. What a fine feeling this was, cleaning a conquest's gory remains from his weapon. Part of him wanted to keep some traces of it on the blade, a little trophy in its own right. But a raccoon's blood was hardly worth the space. He would need to save that for the gnome. He wondered if the fiend's blood would be red. Perhaps it was green, like some sort of insect. How disappointing it would be if it turned out to not have blood at all, its insides dry like jerky.

With Alexander cleaned and the bathtub draining, he snatched up his fresh new clothes. As he did, something heavy and moist plopped from his shirt onto the floor. It was dark and long. His first horrified thought was that it was fecal matter. But inspecting it closer, it appeared to be alive. It looked like a snake, with black and white streaks across its body. Then he noticed protrusions jutting from its body—slimy little legs—and went cold. As if sensing his terror, the lizard crawled toward Neville's bare feet. He jumped backward, screaming, slipping and falling to the floor, nearly banging his head against the tub. Before the creature could get the chance to skitter up his legs, he scrambled back onto his feet. He snatched up the rest of the clothes, but then dropped them again when several more lizards plopped out.

Alexander in hand, he ran out of the bathroom, down the stairs and into the crisp daylight, naked as the day he was born.

Neville paced along the front porch, fully clothed again, trying to reclaim his shaken nerves. Even if all the lizards were removed, would he be able to use that bathroom ever again? Thomas was up there now, dealing with the issue just as he had dealt with the rattlesnake. So humiliating. Thomas had found Neville curled up on the porch, a naked mumbling mess.

The exasperated look those dark eyes gave him when he spit out the words "Lizards . . . in the bathroom . . ." would be burned in the blackest, most resentful recesses of his brain. What right did Thomas have to make him feel so foolish?

This was a defeat. It could be called nothing else. To think only moments ago he had felt so powerful. Now the gnome, the one he'd gleefully imagined cowering in its last moments, was no doubt laughing at him. He had been beaten. No, slain! As pathetic as that raccoon. His blood rushed with rage and vengeance. He wanted to destroy, to raze the land. To kill anything and everything. But in the end, what could he actually do? What kind of power did he have? He had nothing. A stick of dynamite without a fuse. No, he was a firecracker without a fuse that had thought it could be dynamite.

He couldn't do this. What a disgusting, pathetic fool, frightened off by slimy little reptiles. What kind of Teuton was he, relying on a native to come swooping in to save the day? No, he was no Teuton. He was no lumberjack and certainly no warrior. He was defective, every bit the aimless clown his father told him he was. Soon Mr. Morton would see Neville the same way. Slitting his own throat with Alexander would be the best thing for him. No, he didn't deserve to be felled by such a magnificent weapon. Perhaps he would be more suited using a woman's comb to do the deed.

Neville eventually lost the energy for pacing and rested along one of the pillars of the porch. Behind him, he heard Thomas step out through the front door. He refused to look up at the man.

"I think I got them all," said Thomas. Though his tone was neutral and uncertain, Neville felt he was gloating. "They were skinks. Haven't seen one of those in a while."

Neville denied him a response.

"You know," Thomas continued cautiously, "if you want to leave, we can provide money for a train ticket."

Neville tightened with anger. Of course Thomas wanted him to leave, then he would be Mr. Morton's only aide and, by proxy, his favorite. What a worm he was. Slimy and slinky as a skink. But the worst part of it all was how tempted Neville was to take him up on his offer.

So, for his own sake, Neville stood up and, without looking at Thomas, said, "Go to hell," and marched back inside the house.

By the time evening set in, Neville's nerves settled. Still, he felt deeply ashamed and sickened with himself. He spent most of his time in his bedroom, that room where a true man had once laid his head. When he heard Morton come home, having apparently been in good enough health to go into town, he was too afraid to face him. It was only after an hour or so of pacing that he finally worked up the courage to leave his room and find Morton sitting in the parlor. The old man seemed contemplative, seated at the edge of the sofa, twisting a cane in his hands and staring at that sweeping Table Creek Treaty painting. When he finally noticed Neville, he laughed warmly.

"You truly do take that axe with you everywhere. Don't you, my boy?"

Neville was relieved that Morton was in a good mood. Perhaps he hadn't heard about the skink incident.

"Come," Morton said, "sit with me."

Neville obeyed, sitting in a creaky wooden chair across from Morton.

"I was thinking about my sons," the old man went on. "In particular, I've been thinking about my youngest, Carl." His mustache shuddered from quivering lips. "You see, I lost him very recently."

Neville felt it best not to mention that he already knew this.

"He had such a bright future. A true businessman and innovator, taken from us in his prime."

Neville felt a jealous pang building but fought to keep it at bay.

"It has been a difficult thing to face," Morton continued. "Some days I've wondered how I can go on. There are times when it seems the world is crashing down. Carl's passing, this curse. It's too much to bear. But these past few days, I've felt healthier and more hopeful than I have in a long time." He smiled at Neville. "You, my boy, are my savior."

Neville's heart lifted. After such a day, this was exactly what he needed to hear, and precisely the man he needed to hear it from.

His spirits rose even higher when Morton added: "I do believe you and I are destined for a long and fruitful friendship."

And that settled everything. Neville hadn't failed. He would not fail, for he and Morton were inextricably linked, eternally entwined, bound by fate. As Morton had said, Neville being here was God ordained, destiny in motion. He was a Teuton, a warrior. Neville would succeed, for failure would be a perversion of destiny, of nature and order. He would no sooner fail than fish would start to walk on land. Everything was part of the plan, even the humiliations and setbacks. They were simply the pieces falling into place for the great move. The gnome was only the beginning. His great work wouldn't end when its head was mounted on Morton's wall and the curse was lifted.

He leaned back in his creaky chair and smiled, resting Alexander against his chest. Neville Gibbons was a force of destiny, and destiny was unstoppable.

CHAPTER SEVEN

THE NEXT TWO MONTHS were trying, but Neville persevered. As the world grew hotter, he grew harder, more resilient, and skilled.

The curse on the house would not relent. The plants continued sprouting up stubbornly and the critters only seemed to increase in number. But he was relentless, too. He killed many prairie dogs, be it with his axe, poison, or his boot. He slaughtered prairie chickens and pheasants and ate them for dinner. Despite Thomas' lackluster cooking, the meat he killed was the tastiest he'd ever had. The skinks and lizards didn't even bother him anymore. He could grab their slimy little bodies and crush them in his hands. He kept hoping another rattlesnake would dare show its ugly head, as he would be ready for it, though none had been sighted since the incident in Morton's room. Sometimes he could still hear noises coming from Caroline's bedroom, that thudding and groaning, and smell that distinctive stink. But his hands were tied. Morton would not allow access to that room. Besides, he was willing to pass it off as a glamour, a trick by his hideous nemesis. It was impossible such a beast might actually be up there. The smell no longer bothered him anyway.

But tolerable as the gnome's curse had become, the fiend still eluded him. He hadn't heard that awful giggle for a long time, nor had he seen those massive eyes. Perhaps it was scared, hiding from him. What an exciting thought! But it was surely still there. Its presence was felt through the curse, the animals and plants, not to mention the damned rashes he kept getting, the sting of wild parsnip. But the rashes meant nothing. He fought them back with balms and creams. He no longer minded going into town for errands; it didn't matter what the townspeople thought of him. Before long, the glares and snickers and gossip subsided.

Life settled into a fine routine. Breakfast with Morton, at least when the man wasn't indisposed. They no longer ate outside, as Morton's beloved bur oak grew worse and worse. The tree was now more brown than green. But in the comfort of the dining room, the man would talk on and on, telling Neville stories of his boyhood or his impromptu governorship of the Nebraska territory, or his time on the Cleveland administration, or of the countless great and strange men he'd met. Sometimes Neville was captivated, sometimes he barely listened at all. It only depended on how interesting the story was. When Morton spoke about his wife and children, Neville never paid attention.

As for lunch and dinner, Neville was sometimes joined by Morton, but usually ate alone, sitting in that large dining room with its ticking grandfather clock and stained glass windows. He liked to pretend he was lord of a castle, feasting alone in his great dining hall.

Some evenings, he and Thomas would drink together. Given how their first visit had ended, the men rarely spoke, unless the drink particularly hit Thomas hard, and he recalled an old joke or an amusing anecdote. The filthy jokes and crude stories reminded Neville of the banter at the lumber camps that he had never been invited to take part in. But when Thomas told them, they were just for Neville. In those moments, he truly seemed to belong. He wished he had his own jokes to share, but the only ones he had were never filthy enough to match Thomas's. They were too polite, too socially acceptable: like the man telling his mother he had two holes in his trousers——the ones he put his feet through. The true joy of those evenings with Thomas, however, was the whisky and not having to drink it alone. Of course, Neville didn't always mind drinking alone. There were nights when he would finish off his day—especially if he'd had a kill or two—in the parlor with a glass of bourbon, staring at the Table Creek Treaty painting as if it were a still play put on for his amusement.

Only one thing gave him fear: the anticipation of his father's letter. The morning after Morton told Neville they were destined for a long and fruitful friendship, the lumberjack had been emboldened to write to his father. It was filled with all the usual courtesies: *I trust you are well. How is mother doing?* But much of the letter had been committed to explaining he was under the employ of J. Sterling Morton—*Perhaps you have heard of him?*—an entrepreneur and statesman. He took care to state that the undertaking paid quite well, and he was willing to send any money his father may need. It had delighted him to imagine his father's reaction. No doubt the man had spent these past years uncertain his youngest son was even alive. But to learn that he not only was living but thriving under the employ of such a prestigious figure—his eyes would pop from his skull with fury! Neville had felt so excited after sending the letter off that he had to stop and pleasure himself behind the nearest tree. But as the days went on, he became nervous. It was such a strange thing, perhaps an old residual habit. His father could do nothing to him, not if Julius Sterling Morton had anything to say about it. Yet his anxiety grew, especially as weeks became months without a response. Perhaps his father knew the agony the anticipation would cause.

He tried not to focus on the letter, or his father. The gnome took priority. The shipment of bear traps finally arrived, and Neville spent an entire day setting them up around the perimeter. Thomas helped a little with this job. Neville was starting to see that man's usefulness, and he was quite willing to engage in most tasks. He had even given in and agreed to wash Neville's clothes every two weeks once the lumberjack's stink became too aggravating for him.

Everything was looking up for Neville. He was on the path to glory. Let his father try his worst, or perhaps try nothing at all, it didn't matter. He didn't matter. The old bastard would matter even less once Neville held the gnome's bloody head in his hands.

It was a sweltering June day, but Neville was largely shaded by trees. He patrolled the grounds, checking his still freshly laid traps. None of them had caught anything, to his disappointment. The only monster he encountered on his patrol was that smirking son of the grocer, William. His two minions were apparently elsewhere, perhaps being made to do something useful, and he was forced to entertain himself.

"I'm General Custer," the boy shouted at Neville. "Prepare to die, savage!"

But the ugly little child ran screaming when Neville swiped Alexander into the air, shouting: "Get away, you!"

He re-covered most of the traps with leaves and sticks. Thomas had told Neville to be careful about that, particularly since *he* didn't want to accidentally step in one of those traps. The gnome was no doubt perceptive with those giant eyes. If there was any chance of these traps working, they would have to be more hidden.

With the task complete, Neville walked back to the house, disappointed but undeterred. Every day, he had to remind himself that he was on the path of destiny. It was a slow track, but one that required patience. When his time came, it would be magnificent. Besides, Mr. Morton believed in him. However long his time took to come, the wait would be okay so long as he had Morton.

This was why he felt so horrified when he came back to the house to find the old man in the parlor, seated next to a younger, familiar-looking man.

"Ah, Neville," Morton said brightly. "We were just discussing you. I would like you to meet my son, Joy."

He hated the way Joy Morton sat, that upright and pompous posture with his hands on his lap, like an awkward child next to his dignified father. He also hated the way Joy looked: a young, perverted mirror of the senior Morton, lacking the seriousness or weariness of his elder. He had a dark, well-groomed mustache, undergirded by the same unappealing smile as his father's, except he chose to wear it constantly. Neville hated his clean clothes. He probably did his own laundry. What kind of name was "Joy" for a man anyway?

"It's a pleasure to meet you," Joy said. Neville hated his voice. It had the same authoritative cadence as Julius Sterling's, but with the untouched arrogance of youth. He reminded Neville of his brothers, those "respectable" men with their "respectable" lives. It was certain Joy would have been one of the boys who bullied Neville in primary school or who mockingly condescended to him in college.

"A quiet fellow, isn't he?" Morton said when Neville didn't reply.

Joy glanced at Alexander. "Were you chopping wood?"

Morton laughed. "Oh my, no. He carries that axe with him like I carry my canes."

"Oh?" Joy shifted with discomfort.

"Sit with us, why don't you?" Morton said to Neville.

As he wished. As Neville sat across from the two Mortons, Joy continued nervously eyeing Alexander.

"Would you care to put that away, Mister . . . "

"Gibbons," Morton interjected. "And it is no matter."

Neville's affection for the older Morton cooled his resentment of the younger. What J. Sterling Morton said went, and his femininely named son would have to live with that.

"Very well," Joy said. His anxious acquiescence made Neville giddy.

Although the lumberjack had been invited to sit with the Mortons, they proceeded to converse as if he weren't in the room. Granted, they spoke of things about which Neville would have little to say: Joy Morton's "salt" enterprise for one thing. The way Joy went on and on about salt, one would have thought it was the most fascinating and valuable substance in the world. The young man seemed to hope his company would become a household name. When deigning not to discuss the wonders of salt, Joy spoke of his late brother, Carl, particularly the question of what to do with his corn starch business. Morton only listened to these details in solemn silence. At some point in his rambling, Joy was interrupted by the sound of scratching beneath the floors.

"What on Earth is that?" he asked.

Neville was pleased to answer, hoping it would mortify Joy further. "Prairie dogs."

This response had the desired effect. Joy's thin face paled. "Prairie dogs? Those are rodents, are they not? My god." He looked around the room. "This place has gotten even worse since last I was here. Father, I think perhaps it might be best for you to move to Illinois."

Morton immediately shook his head, as Neville hoped he would. "Impossible."

"Carrie and I have discussed this at length, and we both agree that it would be best for you to live closer to family. I understand this is a bit sudden, and I apologize. Certainly you ought to have time to think it over. I would have written to you but thought it best we discussed this in person.”

“I appreciate your offer,” Morton said, “but this is our family’s house. Our legacy.”

“I have no wish to get rid of the house,” Joy said. “But it could use quite a bit of fixing up. Perhaps not only that, but it could be expanded. I actually have a lot of ideas for that. It’s the twentieth century now, and this should be a twentieth century mansion. We could put in a foyer, add a third floor, a bowling alley perhaps.”

“Perhaps,” says Morton. “But none of that can be done until the creature is killed.”

“Creature?” Joy’s first reaction was confusion, which quickly gave way to bemusement. “You’re not talking about that ‘demon’ of yours, are you?”

“Of course,” Morton responded tersely. “That monster has cursed our family. It will not be stopped until its death or all of ours!”

Neville almost laughed at seeing the weak young man shrink into a hunched husk at his father’s anger.

“I am sorry if I offended you,” Joy said meekly. “But please appeal to reason. I cannot picture any creature having the power you claim this one does. Especially a creature that nobody except you has seen.”

“Someone else *has* seen it!” Morton pointed to Neville.

Joy didn’t even take a moment to humor the lumberjack’s input. “Regardless,” he said, “we are Mortons, are we not? Must we let some boogeyman hold us back?”

Morton leaned on his cane and pointed a condemning finger in Joy’s face. “You’re the one who wants me to leave!”

“I want you to *thrive*,” Joy stopped shrinking and sat upright, apparently growing bolder. “This is not a healthy place for you right now. It’s probably not a healthy place for *anyone*. Are you thriving here? I don’t think so. Certainly not in the way I’ve always known you to. Call it a demon’s curse or whatever you will, but there is something wrong with this house. I at least agree with you that we must get to the bottom of it. Once we do, we’ll fix this old house right up. We’ll make it better than ever! But in the meantime, why don’t we get you somewhere you can be more comfortable? Besides, you won’t be alone in Illinois like you are here. You’ll have me, Carrie, our children—your grandchildren! I believe your health will improve out there. You'll become right as rain in no time."

Neville hoped Morton would continue arguing, hold his ground, cut Joy down to size, perhaps even throw the fool out of the house. Instead, the old man frowned and stared at his cane ponderously. "I have been out of sorts here."

"Nothing that a change of scenery can't solve," Joy said, patting his father encouragingly on the shoulder.

Neville felt like he was swallowing a ball. It was almost bewitching how Joy had managed to turn his father around on this, and so quickly.

Morton grumbled and shook his head. "But Arbor Lodge . . . "

"Arbor Lodge will always be our family's house," said Joy. "But for now, your health must be the top priority."

"You might be right," said Morton.

Neville's bafflement turned to horror. It was like the son had reverted his father into an obedient little boy.

"Of course," Joy continued, "we need not worry about any of that right away. We can get your affairs here in order first."

"Very good," said Morton.

A silence settled in the room, and Neville felt this was his chance to say something. Yet, he couldn't think of anything. How could he compete with Joy's persuasion? He had no words that could turn Morton back to his side, to convince the old man he must stay in Nebraska. So much for his college education. But he had to say something. If Morton left, that would be the end of his employment. On top of that, the gnome would win. He had to do something, anything. Perhaps if he had more time with Morton— more time with the man than Joy did—that would give him an advantage. It would give him time to build a compelling case.

To see if he had such fortune, he asked Joy: "Will you be staying in town then?"

"In town?" From the bewilderment in Joy's face, Neville knew he had no hope in this regard. "I should think not. I'll be staying here, of course!"

"Of course," Morton affirmed.

There was only one option, then. The only way for Neville to keep Morton here, and to secure his special position, was to kill the gnome as soon as possible.

CHAPTER EIGHT

DINNER WAS AN insufferable affair. Instead of dining alone, Neville was joined by both Mortons. Joy continued to prattle on about salt, his wife, and his children. The sounds of prairie dog scratching became a welcome balm against the man's dreadful voice.

Neville had to excuse himself after Joy said, "Mr. Dailey did a fine job with this chicken. Though it would be good to get a real chef on hand. This house could use a real staff again." What hurt most was the older Morton agreeing without even a glance toward Neville.

The lumberjack tossed and turned that night with angry thoughts storming through this head. Everything had been looking up before Joy Morton's arrival. But now that he was here, it felt again as if Neville no longer belonged. This was beyond the pale. It would not do.

When it was clear sleep would not come, Neville snatched up Alexander and headed out to the front porch. On his way outside, he had a fleeting urge to go to the room where Joy Morton slept and acquaint him with Alexander.

The night air was hot but refreshing. A chorus of crickets and cicadas sang to the moon and stars, which shone brightly down on the trees. Neville leaned against a pillar, calmed by these sights and sounds, his mind emptying. But just as his eyes began to close, they were snapped open by a sound cutting through the insect concert. An ear-piercing scream. It was vaguely human yet sounded like no man or woman he'd ever heard. It was a different kind of creature.

Perhaps *the* creature.

Though barefoot and in his pajamas, Neville was too excited to go back inside and dress. If one of his traps had snagged the gnome, then he couldn't spare a second and allow it the chance to get away. There wasn't even time to put on his boots. He needed to seize this victory, a victory for civilization, for his Teutonic legacy. A victory for him.

He leapt from the porch and charged into the woods, letting the moonlight guide his way. The scream echoed out again, giving Neville a beacon to follow. Sticks and rocks stung his bare feet, and he was nearly tripped several times. He tried to keep to the ground that wasn't covered in too much grass or brush. Getting caught in one of his own traps was the last thing he wanted.

The pained screaming and wailing continued. It gave him strength, his body radiating with excitement and joy at hearing the agony of his hated foe. He honed in on the noise like a predator, letting it grow louder with every step he took. He was hungry, the kind of hunger that couldn't be sated by a thousand meals. The silver-lit world was turning red.

When he finally saw the creature—a grotesque shadow staring at him with glinting white eyes, gaping in horror—he did not hesitate to swing Alexander with as much force as he could. It was a perfect strike. The creature let out one last pathetic whine before it was silenced forever, its head flying from its body. Neville felt the warm blood coat his body, which only heightened his frenzy. He struck again, this time aiming for the now headless body, then again and again. Its bones crunched with each blow, the squelch of its flesh like honey pouring through Neville's ears. The monster's body became a meaty fountain, spraying tepid juices everywhere.

It was not satisfaction that finally stopped Neville, but exhaustion. By then, the creature was a wet pulp of limbs and blood and innards. Just like that raccoon, his first kill. The world was silent around him, no crickets or cicadas sang. All he could hear was his haggard breath. When his breath settled, he turned his blood-coated face to the sky and howled like a wolf.

He had done it. He was worthy.

Cleaning up the body would have to wait. Despite the excitement buzzing through him, he was drained. All he took with him was the head, which he stuffed in a sack from the kitchen upon returning to the house. He couldn't wait to show it to Morton first thing in the morning.

As soon as he entered his room, he tossed the sack aside and plopped into bed. He didn't care about the dried blood covering his clothes, skin, and now his sheets. Morton would understand, everyone would understand.

As he lay in bed, he rested Alexander over his chest. Like him, the axe had been baptized in blood and deserved a warrior's sleep. As his mind began to drift, he heard the prairie dogs scuffling beneath the floors. Did they know? Were they aware that their king was dead? He almost felt pity for the creatures. They could scratch and scuttle and bark all they wanted, but they were doomed. He had doomed them. *He* had.

He smiled, savoring the feeling of the gnome's bodily sap clinging to his clothes and skin. Only moments ago, he'd thought he was running out of time. But destiny prevailed. Unlike the prairie dogs, he had no pity to spare for poor doomed Joy Morton. Now that the curse was quelled and the demon slain, Julius Sterling Morton would return to full health, with his palace restored. Joy would slink off back to Illinois, but Neville would remain. He would become Mr. Morton's right-hand man.

He imagined the dining room filled with prestigious guests: President McKinley, Vice President Roosevelt, former president Cleveland, perhaps some kings and princes from the great nations of Europe, a general or two. At one end of the table would sit Morton, at the other end, Neville. They would have a delicious feast, prepared only by the world's finest cooks, and there would be servants waiting on them. All the while, hanging on the wall above them, would be the gnome's hideous head.

Joy Morton would be one of the servants, pouring wine for his father and Neville and the other men.

"That's enough, boy," the great Theodore Roosevelt would say to Joy, after the buffoonish young man overfilled his glass. Then the vice president would turn his attention to Neville. "What a fine kill! I can imagine such a creature putting up a fight."

"Not enough," Neville would say, sparking uproarious laughter.

"A strange and elusive creature, wasn't it?" Mr. Morton would add. "But mortal, in the end."

"And what is next for the great Neville Gibbons?" President McKinley would say.

"Why? Are you offering him a job?" some foreign prince would say.

"It better not be mine," Roosevelt would chime in, and the room's occupants would laugh.

"Perhaps mine, one day," would add McKinley. All the men would nod approvingly.

As flattered as Neville would be, he would shake his head. "I will leave politics to those who can stomach it. My place is in the forest." He would raise Alexander, which all the men would gaze upon with awe.

Just as his imaginary McKinley began to comment on how admirable it was for a hero such as Neville to continue doing the hard but noble work of a lumberjack, he fell asleep.

It was still dark when Neville awoke, the morning only a bluish tint peeking lazily through the windows. He would have slept more, but he felt like a child waking up on Christmas day. No doubt it would still be some time before Morton awoke. But Neville was so eager to announce his victory, he needed to prepare for the moment.

Firstly, he supposed it was best to make himself presentable. He went to the bathroom, changing out of his bloody pajamas and into real clothes. At the same time, he washed the blood off his face and hands. It was melancholic, washing away the glory of his kill. Yet the true glory was in that sack downstairs.

The head.

He hoped it wouldn't be too horrific for Morton's dignified sensibilities. But whatever it looked like, a true man would no doubt have the strength to face it. Of course, Neville didn't really know how ugly the creature was, did he? He hadn't actually gotten a good look at it.

Rain was trickling against the house by the time he returned to the bedroom. The sack sat on the floor, waiting for him. It made sense, he supposed, that he take a look before presenting it. As he opened the sack and reached inside, a small trickle of fear went through his body. But he reminded himself that he was a man. A lumberjack. A warrior. A Teuton. Even if the head came to life and bit his hand, he would handle it with courage.

Nothing bit him when he got a grip on the damp, scruffy hair. It was a small head, fitting in his hand like a melon. An unsurprisingly small and narrow cranium, befitting a lower race. It was already taking on a putrid stink. If it was to be preserved and mounted, they would need to act quickly. He moved to a window, bringing the head into the dim light. It looked nothing like he'd expected. Its skin was pale and though the face was rather ugly, it wasn't quite the hideousness he'd anticipated. The eyes were smaller than they should have been. Its shapes and proportions were almost human.

Outside, the rain hissed louder, popping along the windows and walls. The longer he looked, the more the creature's head began to look familiar. Was it the snubbed nose? The crooked mouth? Or maybe the . . .

His body seized up. He dropped the head and fell onto the floor. Oh god. This was not the gnome's head. The lifeless, terrified face that stared at him through the dimness was that of a boy. William, the grocers' child.

CHAPTER NINE

THE EARLY MORNING rain shower proved to be a gift from God. It washed away much of the blood from the gruesome scene of William's death. It also softened the soil so Neville could dig a hole in which he buried the remains, the trap that had caught the boy, and Neville's bloody sheets and clothes. This would at least be a temporary solution. That night, he would return and toss everything into the Missouri river, which ran close to town. The sun was out by the time he filled in the hole and covered the area with as many sticks and debris as he could. There didn't seem to be any witnesses. The world around him was empty but for the trees, the sun, and the rain dew. Yet he couldn't shake the feeling that he was missing something. He couldn't identify what, no matter how much he tried. His mind was blank, an automaton propelled by fear. He was soaked, covered in mud and filth and exhausted. He had to return to the house. Come night, he would finish this.

The house was silent. It appeared the Mortons had finished their breakfast. He wasn't hungry anyway. Either they had returned to their rooms or had gone off somewhere. This was good, as seeing him in such disarray would only raise questions. He quickly paced to his room and slid the muddy shovel under his bed to make sure nobody got to it before night. Dread rang through his body like a church bell. Dread that someone had seen him, seen what he had done. Retribution would soon come. No amount of bail would save him then. Who would want to pay a child killer's bail? But there would be no bail. Killing William would earn him the death penalty. No doubt Mr. Morton himself would find this act unconscionable. What would it matter that it had been a mistake? That it had been a trick of the darkness.

No, perhaps it had been a trick of something even more sinister.

Upstairs came the heavy thudding in Caroline's room, and that wretched stench. Beneath him, the prairie dogs scratched about. He noticed new grasses had sprouted all over his room, green and brown spears bursting from the wilting floorboards. In some places yellow and white flowers joined them in their crawl toward the ceiling. Wheat-like tufts smothered the feet of the dresser, bookshelves and bed. A few flowers were somehow even growing on the bookshelves, nestled among the crumbling old pages. Grasshoppers clung to the walls and hopped about the floor. The quilt of the bed was dusted with seeds, and he could feel them floating in the air, swarming into his nostrils. How had the room fallen to this? Had it been this way just moments before? He couldn't ponder this long before his skin began to burn and itch. He looked down at his forearm, where a trail of red bumps rose to his wrist. Damned rashes. He felt them everywhere: his neck, his arms, legs, stomach, chest, and even his back, where he couldn't reach. As he went into a frenzy, scratching himself raw, the creature upstairs bellowed and the scraping beneath the floor erupted, harmonizing with the fingernails against his skin.

He felt like a fool, hopping around the room, clawing at his body. Of course this was all the gnome's design. Morton had told him, his very first morning here, not to underestimate the creature's depravity. Apparently, he hadn't taken that to heart. What a stupid fool he was. Now the gnome had gone too far. It had the blood of a child on its hands. Even worse, it had made Neville its weapon. If this were ever found out, he wouldn't just be put to death, he would be forever scorned by the world. That was why he would make sure it wouldn't be. That wouldn't be simple; no doubt the parents and much of the town were already looking for the boy. Unless they didn't care after all, but he couldn't count on being so fortunate. He would have to hope that his job cleaning the scene had been thorough. It just needed to be enough until nightfall.

Thank god for the rain. That proved that destiny was still on his side, didn't it?

The itching began to die down, but by then his skin felt like it was on fire from all the scratching. In places he even felt blood trickling down his skin. He no longer heard the behemoth upstairs, but the prairie dogs continued their ceaseless clamor. He rushed about the room, snatching at the grasses and flowers. He was able to tear a few of them, but not uproot them completely. Even the flowers on the shelf were firm, strong, as if they had been rooted here for hundreds of years. He felt helpless. He wanted to scream and sob and vomit. But he had to stay calm, and in many ways that necessity made it even worse.

That idiot child. His stupid, irresponsible parents, too. They had played right into the gnome's hands and Neville was suffering for it. Where was the justice in that?

Giving up his battle with the plants, he sat on the floor and buried his head against his knees. As he sat in this fetal darkness, rocking back and forth, he felt something slimy brush against his heel. It was a skink, crawling along his feet. Another taunt. He wouldn't accept this. He snatched the creature and squeezed its squirming body with both hands until its eyes and tongue burst out and the squirming ceased.

Perhaps he had underestimated the gnome and its tricks. But the gnome underestimated him as well. It would pay . . . for all of this.

All Neville wanted to do was confine himself to his room all day. But that wouldn't do. He needed to go out and act as if everything were normal, as if it were just another day. William's disappearance would no doubt be the news of the day for such a small town, so Neville didn't want to direct any undue attention to himself. Besides, the gnome probably wanted him to spend his days bedridden. That would be a victory for it. But the gnome wouldn't win. So he spent the day pacing the grounds, particularly returning to the spot where the gnome's vicious crime had occurred, making sure that William's temporary grave was undisturbed and cleaning any remaining residue.

The day heated up, and the steamy rain made the world feel like one of those saunas the Finns liked to use. But Neville persisted. Only once did his bodily needs get the best of him, and he had to return to the house to scrounge himself a quick lunch. Otherwise he patrolled the grounds vigilantly.

ANTHONY ENGEBRETSON

Everything was surprisingly quiet around the Morton mansion. At no point in the day did worried townspeople come to search the place. Perhaps they didn't care after all. This theory was disproven, however, mid-afternoon, when he found Joy Morton and Thomas Dailey standing near the dying bur oak. Despite their differences—Joy's lighter skin, smaller stature and his finer clothing—they stood and spoke like equals. The sight filled Neville with resentment.

"That's just awful," he heard Joy say, "I do hope they find him."

Thomas, who was leaning against a garden hoe, shrugged. "I'm sure he's fine. Boys get up to all kinds of things. He could be stuck in a log somewhere."

"Indeed," said Joy Morton. Then he laughed. "I remember when I was a boy . . . "

Neville couldn't stand to listen anymore. Joy Morton was such a pretender. What did he care what Thomas knew of his childhood? It was evident Thomas didn't even care.

Come late afternoon, the scene of William's death remained undisturbed. Neville felt more and more at ease; perhaps things would work out. As long as William's remains were on the grounds, he wasn't truly safe, but once they were in the river, his hands would be clean.

He saw Joy Morton again near the carriage house, this time alone, strolling lazily beneath the trees. Obviously, the man had nothing to do. Such a useless existence. Here he was strolling, meanwhile his precious salt enterprise was likely no worse off. But in this moment, there was something odd about the man. He was mumbling to himself. The words were indiscernible, hardly sounding like English. It sounded like he was uttering an incantation of some kind. Then Joy caught Neville's eye, and a deep dread surged through the lumberjack's body. The bright gaze locked him in place, like a spell. After what felt like hours, and without so much as a nod to Neville, Joy looked away and continued his stroll, releasing Neville from his hypnotic glare. Now freed, Neville retreated into the woods.

Maybe there was more to Joy than he had thought, something darker and more sinister. The mumbling, maybe that truly *had* been an incantation. But for what? To protect the house? Or maybe . . .

Neville's ceased his retreat, his body constricting by his next thought.

Joy was cursing the house.

These thoughts were absurd, even to him, but he couldn't bat them away. He remembered how elusive the gnome had been, how clever, despite being such a savage, low-born being. Could such a thing truly be so elusive? Or did it serve a higher power? Perhaps the gnome didn't even exist. It was just a shadow puppet, its perverted dance guided by the fingers of its cowardly master.

No. The idea was still so absurd. Even if Joy had such power, he had no motivation to destroy his family's home. As much as Neville hated the man, he couldn't imagine Joy doing something so despicable.

But then Neville remembered what he had said the day before.

"I have no wish to get rid of the house. But it could use quite a bit of fixing up . . . It's the twentieth century now, and this should be a twentieth century mansion."

What if, in his desire to claim the house and the land for himself, he had to make it undesirable to his father? Unlivable even? A genius plan, if sickening. And to achieve it, he learned some arcane sorcery and hexed the house. That also explained why he was so desperate to have his father come with him to Illinois.

Neville's hatred for Joy Morton was now the strongest it had ever been. He wanted to track the man down and do to him what he had done to William. No, what *Joy* had done to William.

Yet at the same time, he was excited. Imagine what Mr. Morton's reaction to this would be. Perhaps he would disown Joy on the spot. Watching that unfold would be far more satisfying than mutilating Joy. Maybe all of Mr. Morton's sons were in on it, and the old man vowed to disown them all. Meanwhile, his love and affection for Neville would grow.

But he was getting ahead of himself. Neville would need proof. Of course, Morton would need something incontrovertible if he was to believe his own son's deception. So, the question was, where to start?

Neville thought back to earlier when he had seen Thomas and Joy talking. There was a possibility that Thomas was in on this plot too, somehow. Joy's little collaborator. Could Joy be using some kind of perverse native magic that Thomas had taught him?

That first night Neville had a drink with the man, Thomas had said, "Or maybe your gnome just liked things the way they were before all the big cities and the big trees." Not to mention all that talk of "retribution" for what white men did. The resentment in Thomas's tone had been palpable; a poisonous anger that the land had been taken from his people and altered.

So, Joy Morton was offering him vengeance then. What a disgusting plot.

But, Neville reminded himself, though he knew in his soul he was right, he lacked evidence. Gathering proof likely wouldn't be easy. Furthermore, he didn't know the extent of Joy Morton's power, so caution was crucial.

The best place to start, he decided, would be with Thomas. After all, he already had an in with the man. So, the next time they drank together, Neville would stay sober. There would be quite a bit to discuss.

After such a horrific morning, things were looking up. Coming to such an incredible realization made Neville feel like the detective from those British novels he'd heard so many rave about.

He had to stay focused. As delightful as it was to imagine Joy Morton discarded by his father before being hanged for the death of William, as of now, in the eyes of the world, that blood would be on Neville's hands. Disposing of those remains was of the utmost importance.

It was also necessary to make sure Joy didn't know or suspect that Neville had caught on to his plot, assuming the man actually had a plot and Neville wasn't just under a particularly potent "spell".

No, of course there was a real conspiracy at play. It made too much sense. When a man had a gut feeling, he trusted that feeling no matter what.

To throw off any suspicion, Neville dined with the Mortons that evening. Much of their discussion surrounded the usual dull affairs, family and salt and the sort. But at one point, Joy brought up the subject of William's disappearance.

"Dear god," said Mr. Morton. "Do they have any idea where he might have gone?"

Joy shook his head. "Apparently the boy has been known to

sneak out at night on occasion. They believe he might have gone south, along the river. He's been known to wander down there."

Neville kept his excitement contained. This was good. Not only did this throw off any reason for townspeople or law enforcement to search Morton's grounds, but now he knew where to drop the remains. If everyone was searching south, he would go north.

The elder Morton was mortified. "They don't think he fell in, do they?"

"It's a possibility. Of course, many prefer not to say it, especially not in the presence of the parents."

"Of course."

"We can only hope he just got lost. Perhaps they will find him wandering around Iowa somewhere." With that, Joy gave Neville a glance. Brief though it was, it sent a tremor down the lumberjack's spine. Was that a knowing look? A jeer?

"Truly awful," Neville said, as if he'd heard this news the first time. He couldn't tell if the elder or younger Morton believed this reaction genuine, as neither man regarded his comment. Instead, they moved the conversation to other matters. Neville clenched the handle of the axe resting faithfully on his lap. Since Joy Morton's arrival, he had felt the most invisible he'd ever felt since leaving San Francisco. Yet the tides would turn soon. Very soon.

Once night came and all were asleep, Neville made his move. It was a cloudy night, so the moon and stars would be no allies. He had to carry a lantern. Fortunately, he knew exactly where to dig up the boy, the location practically burned into his mind. As he dug into the spot he knew intimately, he suddenly feared that the body wouldn't be there, that Thomas or someone else had found it. But sure enough, everything was there, waiting for him: the blood and mud mixed together into a black tar. Once he took everything out, he made sure to fill the hole back up and cover the spot with sticks. Then, using the filthy sheet as a sack to carry the mutilated remains and the bear trap, he hauled everything, along with the shovel, axe and lantern, all the way to the northern bank of the Missouri River. As he passed through town, he made sure to turn off his lantern so nobody could see its glow. Fortunately, this wasn't a major city where just about anyone could be sauntering about at ungodly hours.

Upon reaching the river, its dark waters flowing carelessly, he did not hesitate to hurl the bundled body in. It didn't make a splash, but a heavy plop. And that was that. He also decided to toss the shovel in for good measure. It was likely an unnecessary move, but he didn't want to worry about it. Besides, there were surely plenty of other shovels along the estate. Who would miss it?

The trip back was much easier, though his back, shoulders, and arms ached. It felt good to curl up in bed.

He slept soundly, certain that this chapter had been resolved.

Early in the morning, he woke up with a striking realization that filled him with terror. He thought it had been clever to toss the body in the northern part of the river while everyone was searching south. He'd overlooked one thing, even as it was being demonstrated before his very eyes.

The river *flowed* south.

CHAPTER TEN

O**NLY A FEW** brown leaves clung to the cragged skeleton that remained of the bur oak, hanging like crisp bats along the branches. It wasn't just sad to look at, it was chilling. Thomas thought the tree looked like the hand of a large corpse, bony fingers splayed and reaching for the sky. It would be good to finally have that thing gone. He supposed he'd have to be the one to chop it down. It didn't seem likely the "lumberjack" was going to do the job. That man hardly did anything but kill a few animals and leave dirt, blood, and hair everywhere.

On the other hand, it seemed the man had tried. Closely inspecting the tree, Thomas had found an axe indentation along its trunk. But Neville hadn't cut deep enough to do real damage.

None of that mattered. His bad feeling about Neville had only grown worse over the last two months, but Thomas never would have thought the man capable of doing what he was suspecting. The possibility hadn't even crossed his mind when the boy first went missing. It seemed most likely the kid had gotten stuck or lost somewhere. Or at worst, he'd had an accident and got himself killed. Thomas never hoped for that possibility. He disliked William. The boy was annoying. Still, he was just a kid. Thomas himself had been a little bastard in his day, at least for a time. No, he never wished death on William, especially not one so horrific.

They had found his remains along the southern riverbank that morning, at least most of them. The boy had been chopped into pieces. Chopped with an axe. Even with that information, Thomas would have given Neville the benefit of the doubt, except for one thing. Last night he had looked out his cabin window and had seen the lantern's glow moving along the woods like a large firefly. Carrying it was the small man, hauling a bloody sack about his size.

Thomas had thought, stupidly perhaps, that it was just some animals Neville had killed. But maybe, even then, something in his heart had known it was more than that. And now, the boy's body was found, along with the remains of a bloody sheet.

Yet, there was work to be done, so Thomas did it. Tend to the flowers, dig up weeds, clean the kitchen, as if everything were perfectly normal. He wished his realization had sunk in the moment Joy had told him the news of the body's discovery. He would have told Joy everything. Now the Mortons were away on some excursion. Thomas would have to go and tell the Sheriff himself. But would he be believed? Would they take *his* accusations against a white man seriously? On the other hand, there was little love or respect in the town for Neville. If nothing else, his testimony would encourage further investigation.

It was settled, then. It was better to go to the Sheriff sooner than later. He felt a twinge of sadness for his occasional drinking buddy. But not much. Neville had dug his own grave. Besides, Thomas had had much better drinking buddies in his day anyway, and none of them had ever murdered children.

The only issue was that Thomas was filthy after his weeding, covered in dirt and soil. It was best to run back to his cabin. At least change his clothes, if there was no time to wash up. If he was going to go to the Sheriff with a serious accusation, it was best that he looked "civilized". He didn't want his claim to be ignored, then his hands would be tied unless he could get through to the Mortons later. But if his accusation was unheeded *and* Neville found out he'd made it, his life would be in serious danger.

He felt like maybe it was in danger already.

As he ran back to his cabin, he looked all around. He hadn't seen Neville all day, thankfully, but couldn't be too careful.

He entered his cabin and changed his clothes quickly. As soon as he felt certain of his safety, he heard the door open behind him. He turned to see the scrawny little man standing in front of the doorway, axe in hand, blocking Thomas' only way out unless he could quickly slip through one of the windows. Neville grinned contemptuously under his mangy beard.

"Shit," Thomas grumbled.

The terror on Thomas' face was delightful. It was no doubt the fear of a guilty man who had been caught. Neville's groin tingled with excitement.

"So, here we are my friend," he said, closing the door behind him, axe at the ready. "Tell me what you know."

"What do you mean?" Thomas said, clearly playing dumb as an impulsive last ditch effort.

His coyness didn't work on Neville. "Please don't," said Neville. "Just don't."

"Alright," Thomas said, "I saw you last night. But if you're asking me what I know, I don't know anything."

Neville's stomach dropped. "Saw me?"

Thomas's eyes gaped, as if realizing he had just said the wrong thing. "Yes, but that doesn't mean anything right? It doesn't mean you had anything to do with the boy."

"The boy?" Neville squeezed the axe tighter, bracing for what he would hear next.

"They found him this morning, along the river."

Neville felt like collapsing. What he feared most since his early morning realization had happened. But he had to stay strong. Press onward. Time was of the essence now.

"Listen, whatever happened, I'm sure we can-"

"Be quiet," Neville snapped, steeling himself. "You're the one who's going to be hanged for William's death."

"Me?"

"I caught onto the plan."

"Plan?"

"Joy Morton's plan."

"Joy Morton?"

The lumberjack stamped his foot angrily, making Thomas visibly jolt. Why was he pretending? He was wasting time with this foolish game. Perhaps that was the intention.

"Listen," Thomas said, his eyes shifting to his bed.

"Enough!" Neville said. "I know he's behind all of this. I know that you're working for him."

Thomas shook his head, his skin speckled with sweat.

"Are you the one who taught him his magic?" Neville said, his bloodthirsty eyes piercing into Thomas, demanding an answer. "Or are you just his servant?"

"Magic?"

"Enough of this, a boy's blood is on your hands. But if you cooperate, then perhaps you can get off lighter than your master."

Thomas closed his eyes and took a steady breath.

"Very well," he said, raising his hands calmly. "You're right. I have been working with Joy Morton."

A burst of excitement and satisfaction filled Neville's chest, but he kept his aching muscles tight. He couldn't let this feeling distract him. "You betrayed Mr. Morton."

"What can I say?" said Thomas. "Joy is paying better."

Neville recoiled in disgust. "And did you teach him that magic? The magic he used to curse to his family home?"

"Magic? Oh no, I don't know anything about magic. I just do the donkey work. You know."

"I will need proof of his sorcery."

"Of course," Thomas said, "Absolutely. I can help you get that."

"You can?"

"Oh sure. Come with me back to the house."

Neville suppressed a smile. He was so close to ending this madness. Joy would be ruined and punished. Mr. Morton would be devastated, but he would have Neville to comfort him. In time, the old man would come to realize he was better off.

"We'll go to Joy's room," Thomas continued. "That's where he keeps all of his books and charms."

Nodding, Neville at last let his screaming muscles relax. He had Thomas now. He had won. As he brought Alexander to his hip, Thomas rushed forward and grabbed the axe's handle.

"No!" Neville cried, trying with all his strength to keep Alexander gripped close to his chest. It wasn't enough to pull it completely from Thomas' hands, but he was able to keep it in his own. Thomas wasn't giving in either.

This game of tug of war tossed the two men about the room, grunting and panting hot breath into one another's faces. Neville's arms began aching quickly, yet he still held tight. It was like his own life was tethered to the axe. But strong as he was, Thomas was stronger, and as Neville's grip waned, the larger man's tightened. Thomas gave one last powerful tug, and the axe flew from Neville's palms. Thomas flew with it, the force of his pull throwing him back. The man looked almost funny, stumbling backwards like a drunk dancer. His mouth was cavernous, his eyes popping. It was the face of a man who knew he had no control. When he at last dropped, he looked to Neville like a falling tree, giving way to a lumberjack's axe. It was a beautiful sight. Neville knew Thomas' head would hit the edge of the chest. Thomas appeared to know too, and something in his face seemed to change before the wet crunch came. A calmness, serenity, Neville thought he perhaps even saw an amused smirk there.

When it was all complete, and Thomas lay on the floor, a pool of blood gathering around his head, Neville took a deep breath. He savored the pungent smell of blood and sweat, felt the victorious joy of a warrior who toppled a terrible foe, looking upon his kill with his bloodied axe in hand.

But his axe wasn't in his hand.

At this realization, Neville screamed like a mother crying for her baby. He clambered to the ground, pushing Thomas' limp body away from Alexander. The axe seemed to be intact. Good. Alexander was a strong boy. But the panic coursing through Neville's body wouldn't subside until he held it in his arms. As soon as he picked the mighty weapon up, he knew something was wrong. He heard the snap first. Then time came to a complete halt as he watched the axe's head fall from its body, leaving only a jagged stick in Neville's hand. He screamed again, the horror reverberating through his lungs.

Thomas lay still on the floor, a deep slumber that couldn't be shaken by the lumberjack's howling. Once Neville's scream dwindled to blubbering and sobbing, he tried to put the head back on, desperately hoping something would click it back in place. But with each attempt, the head simply clattered to the ground again. It was useless. Alexander was dead. Even if he could use some sort of adhesive to reattach the head, it wouldn't actually fix anything. It could never serve its proper purpose again.

He howled again, now in grief rather than horror. Even as his voice became sore and hoarse, he continued keening. He felt as naked and defenseless as the day he was born, when his soft body had been ripped from the warmth of his mother's womb and placed into his father's cold hands.

CHAPTER ELEVEN

THE TERROR AND GRIEF never faded, but the paralysis eventually did. Neville had to continue to live. Perhaps he could make everything right. He owed that to Alexander.

Thomas was surely dead. The man laid flat as a board, his head bleeding, and he didn't appear to be breathing. Neville's first task was to bury him. Fortunately, there was a small shovel in the cabin, suitable for digging another grave. The soil near the cabin was stubborn, and Neville wasn't able to dig hardly even three feet deep, but it would have to do. He supposed later he would chop up the body and toss it in the river as well. When realizing he would need a different axe for that task, his soul curled into itself.

But this wasn't the time for that. He had to move on.

He dug a smaller grave for Alexander, one that was shallower, but more cleanly crafted than Thomas's. When the last gleaming vestige of the axe's blade vanished beneath the dirt, he began sobbing. Alexander would never be seen again. Well, maybe one day it would be dug up and placed in a museum. It would stand upon a pedestal for all to see, given the reverence it deserved. All would look at it and say, "This was the trusty axe of the great Neville Gibbons." The thought gave Neville enough comfort to pull himself together.

Upon shuffling back into the house, he found the two Mortons sitting in the parlor as they often did, both fully dressed and dapper. They seemed oblivious to the grasses and flowers bursting out from the floor, furniture and shelves, grasshoppers and crickets flitting about their feet, and the earthy smell in the air. Perhaps they had simply grown accustomed to the madness.

"Ah, Mr. Gibbons," J. Sterling Morton said. The use of Neville's last name instead of his first stung. "We will be dining in town. I trust you can see to yourself? Perhaps Thomas would be kind enough to throw something together for you."

The lack of an invitation stung even more, though Neville would have refused it.

Joy Morton stood, looking contemptuously at Neville's dirty clothes. Neville grimaced back, hoping his face showed just as much contempt. He wanted Joy to look into his eyes and realize his end was near. But if the man came to this realization, he didn't show it.

"You've received a letter," the younger Morton said, handing the envelope in question to Neville.

The paralysis returned to Neville's body. Before even looking at the envelope, he knew it was from his father. He could have screamed.

Not now.

Not ever.

"Do clean yourself up," said the elder Morton to Neville, pulling himself to his feet with his cane. "You'll get dirt all over the house." He spoke as if the house wasn't already being invaded by filth.

"Your axe," Joy Morton observed with surprise. "It's strange to see you without it." The mockery in his tone was subtle; a naive listener might have missed it completely, but Neville knew it was there. Joy was lucky Neville was too weakened by grief and pain to lunge forward and attack.

"Ah," said Mr. Morton, half-interestedly. "What has happened to your little companion?"

"Have a fine dinner," Neville said, rushing back into his room before he could spiral into panic.

As he lay on the bed, catching his breath, he heard the mumbling of the Morton men's conversation. He couldn't hear what they were saying, but he knew they were talking about him. Finally, the mumbling moved from the parlor toward the front door. At the sound of the door shutting, all went quiet. The silence was a balm on his nerves.

Neville stared at the envelope in his hand. He wouldn't dare open it and risk releasing whatever horrors it contained into the room. His father had power, perhaps greater than whatever sorcery Joy Morton possessed. It was doubtless that he had enchanted the letter, and whatever curse it contained was waiting to reach out and wrap its hands around Neville's throat.

He tossed the letter aside. The act gave him a small inoculation of strength and resolve. A true man accepted defeat or oblivion only when his body was cold. His enemies were powerful, but he was stronger. He just needed to keep fighting. He was not a squishy, plump infant, but a hardened man—a Teuton, strengthened by destiny. Warrior? Lumberjack? Those weren't sufficient to describe what he was meant to be. No word was. His foes were weak cowards. He was not. He was going to fight and bite and tear until nothing remained but him and a lake of blood and gore.

Joy's bedroom looked like it had been through a storm by the time Neville was done with it. He searched the clothes, tossing them about; he ransacked the bed, the drawers. There was nothing—no spell books, no magical writings, not even letters of malicious intent. There were boring letters to and from his wife and other family members, business documents, everyday medicines, journals, but nothing interesting. Nothing damning.

Neville paced back into the parlor. Thomas had come to nothing. Joy's room had come to nothing. The proof was obviously well hidden, but where was it? Perhaps it wasn't in the house.

Could it be there was nothing to his suspicion?

He sat on the sofa, clutching his head. No, he couldn't be wrong about Joy. It made too much sense. Or maybe it didn't. In fact, it was making less sense by the minute. But that wasn't right, it needed to.

The scratching beneath the floor returned. That damned scratching. It sounded like millions of them. No matter how many he killed, they just kept coming. From the dining room came a shrill chirp. He glanced over to see one of the prairie dogs, standing on its hind legs beneath the grandfather clock.

"Shut up, you bastard!" he barked back. But the creature was undeterred.

Neville leapt to his feet and charged for the prairie dog, hands gearing to wring its body. But it quickly retreated behind the clock once he was only inches from it. Another chirp came, this time from back in the parlor. The little beast was on top of the sofa, staring widely at Neville. He grabbed a candle holder from the dining room table and hurled it at the prairie dog, but the animal ducked before it could be hit. The scratching became louder and more erratic; the prairie dogs were all frenzied.

"Shut up! All of you!"

His screaming was useless. The scratching continued. Behind him, near the clock, the barking commenced. In the parlor, two more prairie dogs appeared, each standing on different pieces of furniture, barking at him. His itching flared up once again. It was as if the horrible little monsters were also crawling under his skin.

"Stop! Stop!" he jolted back and forth between the two rooms, clawing at himself, dancing to the prairie dogs' tuneless song. His rage was uncompromising, but he was also powerless, which made him angrier. He thrashed and screamed, knocking plates and candles from the dining room table, kicking over chairs, and even knocking over the grandfather clock, which continued ticking modestly even after crashing into the ground.

The loud crash restored some of his senses. He retreated to his bedroom. The scratching in there was no quieter, so he climbed onto the bed, feeling the seeds cling to his clothes, and held his ears tight with his hands.

"Please stop," he whimpered, tossing back and forth on the bed. "Please." The scratching burrowed through to his shuttered ears, so he begged louder, begged the beasts to stop, to be quiet, to leave him alone, to leave forever. His pleas grew until he was screaming incomprehensibly at the ceiling. He was an erupting volcano, howling powerfully, his eyes bulging. But this volcano had no ash or lava, just helpless hot air.

His screaming finally died down, leaving his throat as raw as his skin, and that was when he realized the scratching had ceased. All he could hear was a heavy wind outside. When did that start? It hadn't been windy earlier. It was still light, though night was approaching fast. He could clearly see the photograph of Morton, Cleveland, and the rest of that cabinet, staring judgementally at him as grasshoppers crawled over their faces. He wanted to ask them what he was supposed to do, demand they give him some sign. He even had an urge to fall to his knees and try to summon the spirit of General Denver to save him.

Upstairs, in Caroline's room, came that ever familiar thudding, followed by a low bellow. That thing. That trick. A shadow. Was there a real animal up there? For too long he had simply let it come and go, mostly because of Morton's wishes to stay out of Carrie's bedroom. But now he was sick of it. No more. It was time for it to face him.

As he pulled himself from the bed, he reached instinctively for Alexander, only to feel nothing but his sheets. He fought away the sting. He was alone, but strong. He was a Teuton. He was Neville Gibbons.

Without any more thoughts, he stormed up the stairs and stood before the forbidden door. The knob wouldn't move, locked. The bovine stink was emanating powerfully from the other side. From somewhere in the room, he heard the animal bellow. It was there, he could practically feel its heat. His body rattled with fear, but he wouldn't hold back. He kicked the door, nearly throwing himself backwards. Even with the protection of his boot, his toes were hurt more than the door. But he steadied himself and kicked again, and again. Each time the door cracked a little louder. Finally, it burst inward, nearly hurtling Neville to the ground.

But he caught himself, steadied his body, charged into the room and . . .

There was nothing. No bossy animal in sight. Even the smell had faded, replaced by a dense grassy smell.

No, he couldn't say there was truly nothing, for the room he had just entered wasn't a bedroom. It was a small prairie. There were certainly *remnants* of a bedroom, a bed, dresser, sewing machine, furniture. But they were all encompassed by green and brown grass, smatterings of flowers and weeds. Bees, grasshoppers, and all other manner of insect fluttered about the plants, heedless of his presence. Unless there was a patch of dirt between the house's two floors, he couldn't understand where this all sprouted from. But that no longer mattered. Here it was: alive, wild, unashamed. He could try to pluck every blade of grass from its place, but it would all grow back. Even if he burned the room, the whole house, it would find a way to grow back. It was unstoppable, unconquerable.

He had been defeated before he'd even started.

Only inches from him, there was a coiled brown shape lying in the grass, a trembling rattle raised like a sword. The serpent stared at him, fury in its black eyes. Neville stared back, willing it to lash out, bite him, end him. Bring his miserable failure to a conclusion. But it refused him even that dignity, instead flicking its tongue before lowering its rattle, uncoiling and slithering off, vanishing within the grass.

CHAPTER TWELVE

IT APPEARED THERE was no reason to do anything but read his father's letter. Neville was defeated, and with this defeat came a deep numbness. He had been squeezed of all his juices. He doubted his father's words would have any added effect.

He brought it to the parlor, the room still in disrepair from his earlier outburst. He sat under the great Table Creek Treaty painting and read the letter with General Denver, J. Sterling Morton, the dancing Pawnee and all the rest peering over his shoulder. The only one who wasn't reading along was the mysterious man in the hat, looking elsewhere. The man Neville had once imagined was him. But it was probably someone else. Perhaps it was the one person aware of the futility of their mission, who knew civilization and reason would never defeat the madness.

Neville, his father's letter began.

He could already hear his father's cold, stern voice. The cold bumps popping along his skin revealed that he wasn't as numb as he'd thought.

It has been some weeks since I received your letter. I have been unsure of how to respond. You run off and vanish from us for nearly three years. Do you realize what that did to your mother? The poor woman was so stricken with fear and worry, she became an insomniac.

I, on the other hand, decided it would be emotionally and financially beneficial to declare you dead. Your mother, bless her, refused to agree, holding onto hope to the very end. When I received your letter, proving your mother's hopes true, I didn't tell her of it. I feared it would only cause her further pain. As for me, the letter left me quite baffled. After all this time, all the suffering you left in your wake, you dare write me? I couldn't begin to think of an adequate reply.

But now, I do have a response. Today has been a bitter day. It was the day of your mother's funeral. Yes, she is dead, and I do believe it is from the pain you caused her. Those agonizing days and sleepless nights became too much for her already fragile health.

If you want my response, here it is. I have had enough. All your life you have brought me nothing but shame and embarrassment. I tried, at the expense of my own well-being, health, and finances, to mold you into something worthwhile. But you continued to fail me. When I believed I would never see you again, I never wept. Not in sorrow, at least. Perhaps I wept in joy. I thought the shame was over. Yet deep down, I feared you were out there, continuing to disgrace me and my name. How unfortunate that I had to be proven correct. I have not heard of your "Mr. Morton", but no doubt he is either desperate or an imbecile.

Your mother's death has left a black hole in my soul. I will carry on, however. I know I will, because I have Eric, Colin, and John. None of them take any notice of your absence anymore. This entire family has forgotten you. Once I finish writing this letter and toss yours in my fireplace, I will follow suit.

So, my message is this, and read carefully. Stay where you are. Or go somewhere else. Burn in Hell. I do not care. But do not return here.

He signed the letter not with "Father" but with his name.

Neville was overcome by a fog. He couldn't tell what he was feeling, or if he was feeling anything. He supposed there was relief that the specter of his father would not be coming for him. Not now, not ever. He was free.

But at the same time, he felt cold, sick. It was not quite the grief he felt for Alexander, but a different kind. Not for his mother; try as he might, he couldn't quite soak the news of her passing in. This cold grief was instead for the man who had truly and finally abandoned him. His father no longer haunted him, but now he was missing the ghost. Yet there was more than that. Beneath the dense cold was a burning fire. He hated his father more than ever.

Suddenly, the fire burst forth, parting the fog and burning away everything else. He jumped to his feet, ripped up the letter, and tossed the pieces about. This act didn't even come close to satisfying his anger.

The front door flew open and the Mortons entered. Both of their mouths gaped when they saw the parlor: toppled furniture, torn paper and broken plates scattered about the floor, the felled grandfather clock still ticking.

"What on Earth?" said Joy.

"Mr. Gibbons," Morton said, "what has happened here?"

Neville didn't answer, only stared at Mr. Morton. Those morose eyes were cold, disapproving. The man who once gave Neville hope, pride even, now seemed distant, cruel and unkind. All Neville could see in Morton was his father.

"This is completely unacceptable," Joy Morton said. "You see, father? This is what I was talking about!"

"Indeed," said Morton. The old man leaned on his cane. "Mr. Gibbons, your services are no longer required."

The words were said quickly, with little consideration. They flew past Neville's head. He only continued staring at Mr. Morton's sagging face, which was twisting and morphing into the face of his father. Beside him, Joy stood grinning, the pathetic, dutiful little pup. Such a joke. Neville clutched the handle of an axe that was no longer there.

"You will be compensated for your time here," continued Morton. "And you can stay at this house for one more night."

"Did he put you up to this?" Neville nodded toward Joy, who looked aghast.

"We both believe it is the right decision," Mr. Morton said with a sternness that would have once made Neville shrink. "This place is not good for my health right now. Illinois would be a better environment for me."

Neville stepped forward, which made both Mortons recoil slightly. Their fear satisfied him, yet it was a pathetic sight. So disgusting. He hated them. What had he ever seen in Julius Sterling Morton?

"My boy," Morton smacked his lips. "I must apologize to you. You came to me in a rather strange and difficult time. I was confused. This demon, this gnome; I'm afraid it is something you and I created. It was quite a convenient scapegoat for our troubles. But now the time has come to put the fantasy aside."

"So you're just going to flee? What kind of Teuton are you?"

Mr. Morton's eyes lit up with rage. "Mr. Gibbons, you best not forget yourself."

"Not if you want any compensation," Joy chimed in.

"Shut your mouth, boy!" Neville hollered.

The two Mortons were a mirror of each other, the way they both stood stiff and pale with horror. It was almost funny. These two clowns couldn't stop Neville, couldn't stop his destiny. He was free, he was strong. The curse would be stopped.

He would burn the house, burn the land, the Mortons, burn his damned father and all of his brothers. The fire would kill and cleanse, and through the ashes a new world would rise. He didn't need Mr. Morton by his side. Morton wasn't worth anything, that was clear now. He didn't need President McKinley or President Cleveland or even goddamn Joe Mufferaw. Burn them all. Burn General Denver, too, and all the others in that painting. They hadn't gone far enough. What man had ever taken destiny by the horns and truly conquered the world? None. They always fell short, stayed too clean. They were all cowards.

But Neville wasn't. He was Neville Gibbons. No, burn his father's last name. He was just Neville. *The* Neville. He was free and would not be stopped.

"Perhaps you should leave tonight," Mr. Morton said. "And without compensation, if you continue acting this way."

"And what about Thomas?" Neville sneered, his grin cragged with hatred and anger.

"Mr. Dailey?" Joy interjected. "I think he's hardly relevant."

Neville ignored him. "Will *he* continue working here?"

"Why do you ask?" Mr. Morton said impatiently.

"If you want to keep him in your employ, then you'll need a shovel."

"That's enough," Joy said. "It's time for you to leave."

"A shovel? What in god's name are you talking about?" Mr. Morton said, his cane trembling.

"You'll need a shovel if you want to find him."

The way their faces slowly morphed from confusion to terror—two schoolboys seeing a ghost—was so hilarious that Neville couldn't contain his laughter. The cold, hateful cackle reverberated through the room. What a couple of fools. They didn't understand the world they were dealing with, not like Neville did.

"We need to go to the Sheriff," Joy said to his father.

Morton nodded, still staring at Neville in horror.

"Remember," Neville said to Morton, his smile now a grimace. "I am your savior."

If Morton had a response, he had little time to say it before being ushered from the house by his son. Neville was again alone. He felt even more powerful than the night he'd killed William. He was a titan.

Then he heard a small, distant giggle.

It seemed to come from outside. He peered out one of the parlor windows. At first, he saw nothing through that mass of trees billowing in the wind, the evening darkness spreading over them.

But then, from the top of the dead bur oak, he saw two massive lights—those fiendish eyes, staring straight at him. The giggle came again, this time even louder, riding the wind. The sound carried an air of mockery that hit him like a bullet. Neville again gripped for the ghost of Alexander. This challenge would not go unanswered. The gnome would finally die.

His boots pulverized the grass and dirt beneath him. Those mighty trees that had conquered the prairie shook in the wind. Neville liked to think they were trembling at his footsteps. They would all bear witness to his greatness.

Only when he reached the bottom of the dead tree, which groaned and popped from the force of the wind, did he suddenly feel a pang of fear. He stamped this fear out of himself. It did not belong. He was on a mission from destiny. Burn the trees. Burn the gnome. Burn it all.

He looked up at the bur oak's skeletal branches, from which those enormous eyes stared jeeringly down at him. This gave him strength, bloodthirsty strength. The gnome giggled, and he replied with a furious roar. When the echo of his cry faded in the air, the giggling was gone. Now, he could sense the little monster's fear in his bones, and it gave him more strength.

Burn the gnome. Burn the trees. Burn the land. Death to it all. He was the fire. He was destiny's purging flame.

The tree's bitter groaning grew louder as he mounted and climbed it. The branches poked and prodded at him, demanding he dismount and leave the tree alone. But he would not. After a short ascent up the trunk, he reached the center, where the branches spread from every different direction.

He looked up, trying to find the branch where the gnome was. But he couldn't see it. He shouted for the creature to show itself, to stop being a coward and face him, face inevitability. His shouts were overtaken by the whistle of the wind and the groaning of the flimsy tree. He screamed, as loud as his raw throat would allow. Once again, the sound was overpowered. Throughout his life, he had recurring dreams where he would try to shout at someone as forcefully as possible—usually his father—but the words would always fall flat, as much as he tried. This felt the same way.

But this was no dream. He rocked back and forth, shaking the tree with the wind.

"Come on, you bastard!" he roared.

No answer came from above, but below he heard shuffling. The sound was too inconsistent to be caused by the wind. He looked down to see what it was, expecting the gnome. What he saw instead filled his body with ice. It was the hulking shape of Thomas Dailey. The man stumbled about, covered in dirt, a dazed and haunted look on his face. Whether what Neville saw was real or an apparition, he kept quiet, not wanting to call its attention to him.

Thomas stumbled and fell against the tree. The tree protested angrily, its trunk crackling and popping. Neville's need to stay quiet immediately faded. He tried to shout down at Thomas to move, but his throat had grown so dry that nothing would escape it. Thomas was now leaning his entire exhausted weight against the weakened tree.

As the cracks and pops grew louder, it became clear the tree was going to fall. Neville no longer felt like a titan. He was that terrified boy locked in his mother's wardrobe, his classmates' favorite target of ridicule. The boy who would hide under his bed when his father came home, as if the man would somehow never find him that way. He was a young boy caught in a trap, at the mercy of whatever force would have its way with him. No reassurances, no promise of destiny could shake the terror he felt. He knew he needed to move, to try and scramble down from the tree, but he was paralyzed.

Stay where you are, he heard the voice of Mr. Gibbons, the man who had been his father, say. *Stay where you are. Burn in Hell. I do not care.*

With one last tremulous crack and groan, the tree fell, and Neville hurtled down, down with it. As the trunk hit the ground, he heard a crunch deep in his being. It wasn't the tree or its branches, but his bones. His legs were crushed beneath the trunk, and the jagged branches were penetrating him in what felt like a thousand places: his arms, gut, face. He could feel the earth beneath him quivering, gold and green lances preparing to burst up and rip the rest of him apart. The pain was relentless, his body shrieking out, even as he was completely silent. Yet at the same time, the pain felt so far away. Warm blood trickled down his body, like numerous skinks crawling along his skin. He thought he heard the scratching of prairie dogs again, but realized the sound was coming from him; his shattered ribs grinding against one another as he breathed.

Inside, anger and bitterness and despair roared through him like flames. These fires had nowhere to go, so they burned him from within. When the flames fizzled out, there was nothing left but a charred wasteland. Trapped within this ashen world, he felt nothing but merciless terror. He whimpered for his mother, for Mr. Morton, for General Denver. But only the wind and the crackling branches answered.

Soon, the pain faded. Even the terror dissipated, and the world darkened into nothing. All he felt now were eyes watching him, the eyes of the Gnome, of Thomas, of General Denver, Mr. Morton and Joy and Caroline and Joe Mufferaw. All stood nobly beneath a great tree, observing his savagery. Then they all turned away, letting him fade into thoughtless oblivion as the soil drank his blood.

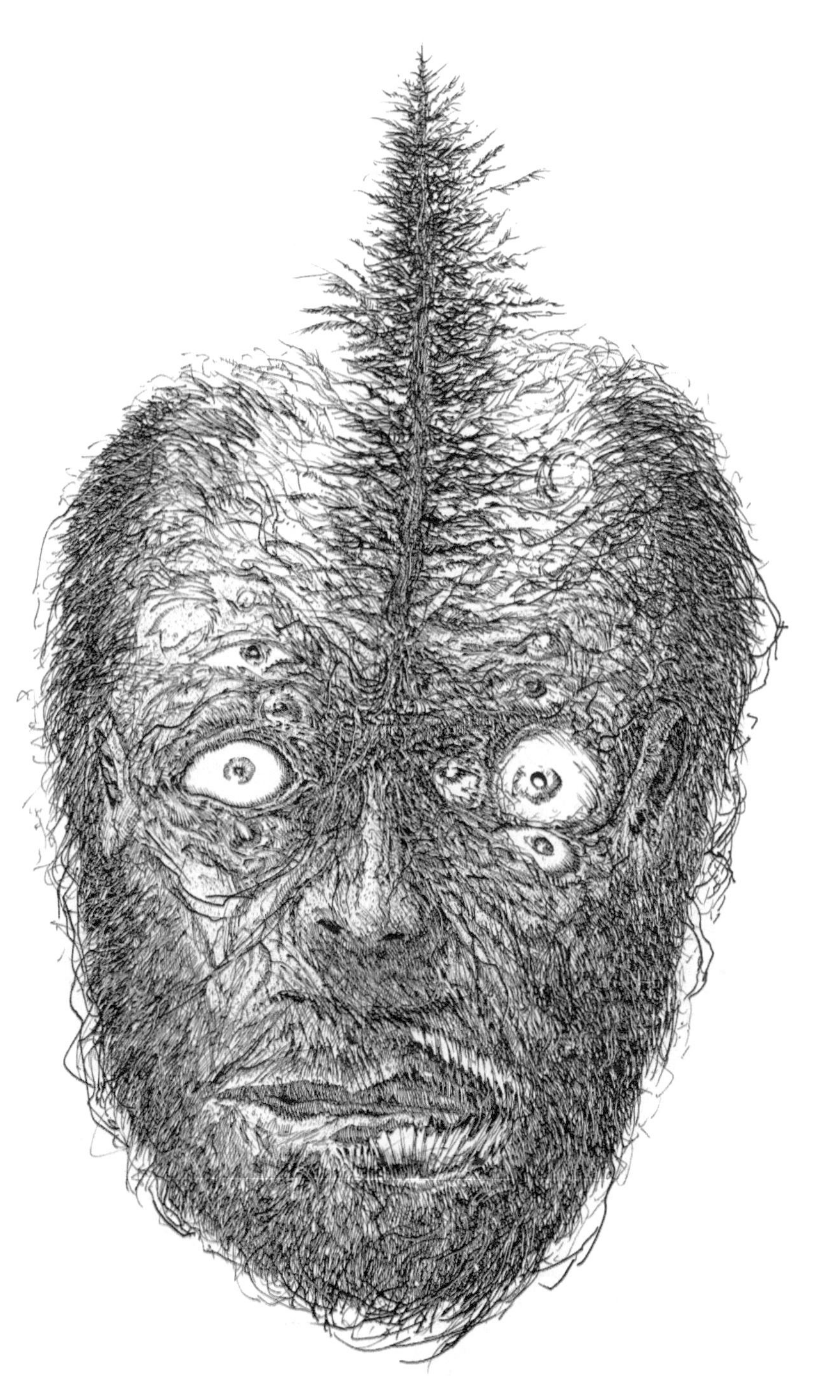

Acknowledgements

I owe much of my historical research on J. Sterling Morton and Arbor Lodge to the Nebraska State Historical Society (History Nebraska) and the Arbor Lodge museum.

Thank you to my parents, Alec and JS, for putting up with my grotesqueries to beta read my book. I also want to thank, now and always, my wife Taylor, who stands by me in all things. Thank you Dylan Relue and all those who helped me make my silly college film "College on a Hill" over ten years ago, which formed the basis of the Neville character.

Of course, I have to thank Matt and Alex at Tenebrous for taking a chance on this strange little book and for going above and beyond in making it the best it could possibly be. This thanks extends to the readers who took time to look at the book to provide their opinions on its sensitive subjects. Thank you as well to Jonathan La Mantia for creating outstanding cover art and illustrations for the book. Also, thank you for reading, and thank you to anyone buying, borrowing, renting, reading, reviewing, promoting and/or otherwise supporting this book.

Finally, thank you to the Great Plains. Though stolen and largely defaced lands, the region still holds an abundance of history and mysteries. There are many—particularly indigenous people—persistently fighting to keep these lands from being further defiled by the powers that be, and even fighting to restore some of what has been lost. To those who think it is all just "flyover country", ground yourself a while. Look past the highways, interstates, fast food stops, and industrial monoculture farms. Underneath it all, the prairie is scratching and whispering, ready to return.

CONTENT WARNINGS

Being a work of mature Horror, a degree of violence, gore, sex and/or death is to be expected.

In addition,
Lumberjack
contains scenes that deal with:

***depictions of racist attitudes that, while accurate with the time period depicted therein, are not aligned with either the author or publisher;**

***scenes of animal death.**

***child death.**

Please be advised.

More information at
www.tenebrouspress.com

ABOUT THE AUTHOR

Anthony Engebretson lives in Holland, Michigan (and sometimes Lincoln, Nebraska), with his beautiful fiancée, two cats and a rescue beagle. His debut novella, *Sair Back, Sair Banes*, was published by Ghost Orchid Press in 2022.

TENEBROUS PRESS

aims to drag the malleable Horror genre into newer, Weirder territory with stories that are incisive, provocative, intelligent and terrifying; delivered by voices diverse and unsung.

NEW WEIRD HORROR

FIND OUT MORE:

www.tenebrouspress.com

Twitter @TenebrousPress
Bluesky @tenebrouspress.bsky.social
Join the Tenebrous Cult on Discord